TENTACLES & TRIATHLONS

LEVIATHAN FITNESS #2

ASHLEY BENNETT

Illustrated by
ALEX CONKINS

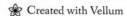

To anyone who wants to be fucked by tentacles...

CONTENT

To view a detailed list of content information for this book, click here. Please reach out to the author with any additional questions regarding content.

AUTHOR'S NOTE

In the original version of Muscles & Monsters, Reece Rollins was the police chief of Briar Glenn. That has since been changed. He is now a supervisor at the parks department.

A special thank you to Tre, Kaylah, Caitlin, Sabrina, and Luna for sensitivity reading and providing feedback. This story was improved because of you.

TENTACLES & TRIATHLONS
PLAYLIST

"Don't Tell the Boys" -Petey
"Drag" -Daywave
"UNDERWATER BOI" -Turnstile
"Fuck June" -Sipper
"Dear To Me" -Electric Guest
"Boys Don't Cry" -The Cure
"Age of Consent" -New Order
"This Charming Man" -The Smiths
"Love Will Tear Us Apart" -Joy Division
"Close To Me" -The Cure

Listen on Spotify here.

PROLOGUE

REECE

Age 10

"Gods dammit," my father grumbled, his eyes focused on the smoldering embers in front of us. "We're getting low on firewood."

"We can grab some from the storehouse in the morning," I offered.

"If you want breakfast in the morning, you're gonna go get us a bundle right now. Take the flashlight and go." He dug through the duffle bag at his feet and tossed me the flashlight.

We were on our monthly father-son camping trip at the campground that sat on the edge of Briar Glenn.

The monthly camping trip I dreaded because it meant alone time with my father.

I flicked the switch on the flashlight and a pale stream of yellow light illuminated the ground in front of me.

"Do I really have to go?"

The thought of walking in the woods alone sent a shiver down my spine.

My father scrubbed a hand over his face and sighed. "It isn't too far. Just follow the trail to the storehouse and get the damn firewood."

"Will you go with me?" I gave him a pleading look, but I already knew the answer.

"Reece Michael. You have been coming to this campground for years. You're a big boy. Now go on."

Wordlessly, I rose from the stump I was sitting on and turned my back on my father.

My lip quivered and I clenched my fists, willing the tears away. There was no way I was gonna let my old man see me cry.

Gods, I hated him. No matter what I did, it was never good enough for him.

I pointed the flashlight in front of me and set off through the woods.

Leaves crunched under my feet, the pitch black of the forest making me grow more and more uneasy with each step. For a spring evening, it was eerily quiet.

The walk seemed much longer than I remembered.

I whipped around, my eyes scanning the darkness for the warm glow of the campfire but I didn't see it off in the distance.

My head spun, the tall trees swirling as they loomed overtop of me, and I dropped to my knees.

I was disoriented.

Disoriented and lost.

There was no way I was going to tell my father about this. He'd never let me live it down.

A twig snapped nearby and my heart raced.

"H-Hello," I stammered, waving the flashlight through

the darkness. "I-Is anyone out there? I'm lost." My voice wavered, on the verge of tears.

Standing on shaky legs, I forced myself to keep moving —to find the storehouse or my father—*anything* to make me feel more at ease.

As soon as I started walking, a shadow bolted in front of the light. I let out a bloodcurdling scream, dropping the flashlight next to my feet.

A fuzzy hand darted out to cover my mouth, the scent of decaying leaves and dust filling my nose.

"Hush, human," a voice that was more like a buzz whispered in my ear.

It leaned in close, it's red eyes staring at me, blinking slowly.

The creature they belonged to was the stuff of nightmares. I could just barely make out its wiry body and the two antennae that shot out from the top of its head.

"What are you doing in these woods all by yourself, little boy?" it asked in that same buzzing tone. "Don't you know these woods are home to monsters?"

The monster let out a shrill laugh that sounded like the buzz of a wasp's nest or a beehive.

My ears rang and tears tracked down my face.

What was this thing and why was it tormenting me?

Again, it leaned in closer, until the fur of its face tickled my nose.

"On the count of three, I'm going to let you go and you're going to run back to your campsite as fast as you can. But if I catch you—well, you don't want to know what happens if I catch you. I never want to see you in these woods at night by yourself ever again. Got it, boy?"

I nodded my head, my eyes wide with fear.

"One. Two. Three."

The moment the creature released me, I snatched the flashlight from the ground and raced through the woods like my life depended on it—because for all I knew, it did.

I didn't turn around to get another look at the monster, I just kept running, scrabbling over twigs and rocks until the glow of the campfire came back into view.

"What the fuck, son," my father bellowed as I collapsed at his feet, my chest heaving.

"The-the monster," I sobbed. "There was a monster in the woods."

My father tsked. "You know there aren't any monsters in Briar Glenn, Reece. Get your ass off the ground. I'm guessing you didn't get the firewood."

Still crying, I shook my head no.

"Gods dammit, boy. I ask you to do one fucking thing and you come back crying about monsters. You're too old for this shit. Get in the tent and go to bed. I can't even look at you right now."

I wiped the snot dripping from my nose and crawled inside the tent.

"Worthless kid," I heard my father mumble under his breath.

The tears continued as I settled inside my sleeping bag. He could think whatever he wanted, but I knew what I saw.

It was an awful, scary monster.

And as much as I hated that monster, I hated my father more.

ONE

Cyrus

I blinked at the bright white canvas in front of me, willing something, *anything*, to inspire me to paint.

My art dealer, Eduardo, had been ringing me nonstop about new pieces, but over the last few months, I'd been at a creative standstill. Everything in my life had become boring. Repetitive. Bland, even.

Being one of the oldest monsters around, and potentially the last of your kind, could do that to you.

My tentacle clenched the paintbrush tighter, almost as if commanding it to move, but it was no use.

"Bollocks." I cursed and whipped the brush at the canvas, coating it with a splatter of yellow paint.

The door to the studio cracked open, and my roommate, Fallon, peeked his head inside.

"Everything okay in here?"

"Fine." I huffed and collected the brush from the floor.

Fallon's beady eyes followed my movements before focusing on the smeared canvas. "Still nothing?"

"Not a damn thing."

He stepped through the doorway, his talons clicking

against the wood floor, and gave me a sympathetic look. *Well*, as sympathetic as someone with a beak and a feathered face could look.

"Are you going to be able to handle tonight? I can find another ride and we can always say—"

"I'll be fine," I said in a clipped tone. "This is important to Atlas and Tegan. As one of his oldest friends, I should be there to show my support."

Atlas had always been there for me when I needed him most. Through my most recent college experience, my move to Briar Glenn, and now in my current existential crisis. After everything he went through with Jade, he deserved happiness, and tonight I'd be there to celebrate with him and Tegan.

Fallon dipped his head in a slow nod and his tail flicked back and forth behind him. I could tell there was more he wanted to say, but for once he didn't press the issue. "Okay then. Well. I should probably start getting ready."

With that, he headed down the hall to his room, leaving me alone in my studio.

I tilted my head from side to side, rolled my shoulders, and let out a deep breath. My frustration and anxiety were getting the better of me, leaving my body feeling sluggish and drained.

There wouldn't be enough time to make it to the gym for a swim, so a soak in the tub would have to suffice.

I shuffled across the hall to my bedroom and into the adjoining master bath. Popping sounds filled the space as the suction cups of my tentacles stuck to the tile floor with my movements. The sticky buggers could be a nuisance, but they had their advantages. I never had to worry about slipping in the shower.

While the tub filled, I stared at myself in the mirror, the

fluorescent lighting reflecting off my skin. I admired the perfect turquoise shade, decorated with deep blue-green stripes and splotches that allowed me to blend into the water. In terms of my appearance, they were probably my favorite attribute.

Unlike humans, I didn't wear clothes. My muscular chest was always uncovered, tapering down into a narrow waist that flared to my tentacles. I had eight in total, but preferred to use six of them for movement, keeping the other two wrapped around my arms. They were quite helpful, serving as extra hands for painting or cooking or whatever task I was undertaking.

Some days I truly enjoyed being a kraken, but others, I felt like a total abomination. Even by monster standards, I was quite odd.

I shut off the tap and used my tentacle to open the jar of raw sea salt I kept on the edge of the tub. I sprinkled a generous amount into the bath and used the strength of my tentacles to agitate the water, dissolving the crystals.

"Mmm," I hummed and slid into the warm, salty water.

My tentacles fanned out around my waist, slithering and sliding with delight. It often felt like we were two separate entities. There was me, and then there were the tentacles acting of their own accord.

While they soaked, I grabbed my phone from the ledge of the tub and scrolled through my social media accounts.

A series of engagement photos of Atlas and Tegan popped up on my feed.

The wolven's snout was scrunched into a happy smile as he stared down lovingly at his human mate.

Simply put: the two of them were adorable.

I was happy for them.

Truly I was.

But, if I was being honest with myself, I was also quite jealous of my friend and the love he'd found.

Being one of the last kraken, the majority of my seven hundred year life had been quite lonely. Other than my friendships, of course.

Sure, since monsters had come out to humans I had more opportunities to socialize, but I worried my presence made humans uneasy.

At this point in my life, it was unlikely that I'd find a mate. And even if I did, would they want to be with me?

I dug the sharp tips of my teeth into my thin lower lip and willed myself not to cry. I was supposed to be replenishing my saltwater stores, not depleting them.

With a sigh, I set my phone aside and submerged myself under the water, allowing the warmth to wrap around my body.

As I floated, weightless, my thoughts drifted back to the photos of Atlas and Tegan.

Would I ever be worthy?

Would I ever find that type of love?

TWO

Reece

"Gods damn!" I whooped as I fought to catch my breath. My lungs burned with each gulp of air I desperately sucked down. I smiled at the time on my watch before throwing my arms up over my head and walking in slow circles.

This was my best run time yet. At this rate, I'd have no problem with the 5k run and 20k bike portions of the Briar Glen Triathlon.

That 750-meter swim though? That was a different story.

Due to my muscle mass and poor form, my swimming prowess resembled that of a manatee. I had no speed or stamina whatsoever.

I either had to take my training to the next level or let go of this pipe dream.

And I wasn't a quitter.

"Struggling there a bit, huh, Rollins?" Jimenez said with a sly smile as he slowed to a stop beside me. The asshole had barely broken a sweat, and that would explain why he finished so far behind me.

"Go fuck yourself, Jimenez," I said with a laugh.

My eyes focused on the round globes of his ass in his tight athletic shorts as he trotted off toward the tennis courts to do his usual cooldown routine.

Javier Jimenez was the most attractive guy in Briar Glenn and he just so happened to be my subordinate at the parks department. More recently, he'd become one of my closest friends. To my dismay, that put him strictly off limits.

I turned away from the tennis court and Jimenez, casually adjusting my cock.

I needed to get laid. *Bad*.

As I palmed myself in public—because I had no fucking self-control—my phone vibrated in my pocket.

My mother.

"Ay, Ma. What's up?" I said as I plopped down on a park bench and tugged my sweaty tank top away from my skin.

"I wanted to make sure you're coming over to Tegan's later." She used that authoritative voice that all moms seemed to take with their children—even the adult ones. "This is important to her, Reece."

I tsked and ran a hand through my sweat-soaked hair, brushing the light red strands out of my eyes. That was right, my sister was having a little get-together this evening. She wanted me to meet the wolven that mated her within the first week of knowing her.

My awkward silence was a dead giveaway of how I felt about the situation.

"*Reece*." My mother's voice was laced with tension.

"C'mon, Mom. I didn't forget. I'll be there."

"You better be on your best behavior, Reece Michael. Atlas is wonderful and we want him to feel comfortable around our family."

"Well, I'd feel more comfortable if he kept his sharp monster teeth away from my sister's pus-"

"Reece!" she bellowed, cutting me off.

I couldn't help but laugh.

"I promise I'll behave."

It was the truth too. I wanted to like my sister's mate, and more importantly, I wanted to improve my strained relationship with her.

Things between Tegan and me had soured since I'd expressed concerns over the monster integration of Briar Glenn. She just hadn't experienced what I had.

As much as I tried to move past it, I was still haunted by the memories of that camping trip from my childhood.

Monsters made me feel uneasy.

Monsters with their sharp claws and beady eyes. Their talons and their tusks. I shuddered at the thought.

"Were you listening to a single thing I said?" my mother asked.

"Sorry, I spaced out for a second. I just finished my run."

"Please try to be open-minded. And you never know, maybe there will be some nice guys there for you to meet."

I exhaled a deep breath and rubbed my sweat-streaked temples. "I don't need you, Tegan, and her mate playing matchmaker, Ma. I'm happy being single."

That wasn't true.

I was fucking miserable, but she didn't need to know that.

"Whatever you say, honey. Love you, see ya later. And Reece, don't forget the veggie tray."

"I won't. Love you too."

I ended the call right as Jimenez sat down next to me on

the park bench. Sweat trickled down his temples and slid along the bronze column of his neck.

Fuck.

"How was your time?" he asked as he lifted his tank top to wipe the sweat from his brow, revealing a sculpted six-pack underneath.

I puffed out a breath and quickly averted my gaze, focusing on a centaur couple playing frisbee in the field across from us. "My best yet."

He gave me that winning smile of his, all straight white teeth and full lips, and shook his head. "Wasn't your bike time the other day your best too?"

"Mhm." I leaned against the back of the bench, cradling my head in my hands before tilting my freckled face up towards the sun.

"And swimming?"

"Damn, dude," I scoffed. "Way to kill my runner's high."

One corner of his mouth tilted downwards. Even when he was frowning, he was still hot as fuck. I needed to get a grip.

"Still struggling?" Jimenez asked.

"It's improving—slowly. I need more time to practice, but it's hard to get down to the lake with our work schedule."

"I feel that, man. You need to join a gym with a pool." He put his arms along the back of the bench and stared at me.

"No way. No fucking way." A chill ran down my spine at the thought of stepping into a gym full of monsters.

"Look, Reece. Monsters are competing in the tri. You're going to have to get over this at some point. Your sister is marrying a monster. He owns a gym with a pool. Might as well make the most of it."

"How would you feel if Selene dated a monster? You wouldn't be concerned?" I knew that Jimenez was just as protective of his baby sister as I was of mine—and the two happened to be best friends.

"Nah, man. If they treated her right and made her happy, that would be enough for me."

It had been twenty-five years and I'd yet to have another experience like that with monsters.

Maybe Jimenez was onto something.

Atlas had been nothing but a gentleman—*gentlewolven* —to my sister. According to my mother, he even went out of his way to make sure she'd be safe during the full moon.

Tegan was happy with him. She was cared for.

That would have to be good enough for me.

CARS LINED the long driveway leading to where Tegan's cottage sat nestled amongst the trees.

Did they invite the entire town of Briar Glenn? This was ridiculous.

I finally found a spot and parked my car. As I walked closer to the house, that's when I saw him.

Atlas.

My baby sister's mate.

He was a towering wall of dark gray fur that deepened to black at the tips of his ears, paws, and tail. Speaking of which, that fluffy tail wagged as he leaned over and gave my sister a kiss. Atlas's ears twitched as I approached and he turned to face me, his bright yellow eyes catching me off-guard.

"Uh, hey!" he said in a deep, gruff voice as he waved a massive claw-tipped hand in my direction.

Tegan turned and gave me a tight smile. "Hey, Reece. Glad you could make it."

I knew Atlas was tall, but holy shit. At six-foot-four, I wasn't used to other people towering over me. The wolven was easily seven feet.

Tegan gave me one of those awkward side hugs and cleared her throat. "Reece, this is Atlas. My mate."

The wolven gave a toothy smile and the sharp, white points of his teeth gleamed in the late afternoon sunlight. "Nice to meet you, bud." He extended a furry hand out to me.

I hesitated, not being into casual touch, before taking his hand in mine and shaking. For being a naturally designed killing machine, he was surprisingly gentle. "Nice to meet you too. Our mom has told me a lot about you."

Tegan glared at me and put her hands on her hips.

"And uh, we're happy to have you as part of the family," I added.

Atlas smiled even wider. "That means a lot to me."

I nodded my head and extended the veggie tray out to him. "I brought the veggie tray."

"Come on, we'll get this on ice and I'll introduce you to some people." Atlas grabbed my sister's hand and motioned for me to follow them.

A warm smile spread over Tegan's face as the three of us walked around back. I couldn't remember the last time I'd seen my sister so happy. And honestly, Atlas seemed nice.

But this wasn't the full moon. In an instant, things could change.

That was the thing with monsters. You could never really tell.

THREE

Cyrus

The beanbag flew out of my webbed hand and careened toward a cornhole board emblazoned with the Leviathan Fitness logo. With a loud thud, the neon green bag dropped into the hole, giving me another three points.

"You've got to be kidding me!" Fallon groaned from the other end of the yard where the cornhole boards were set up. "When you said you'd never played before I didn't expect you to be this good."

I blinked my wide eyes and gave the griffon an innocent smile. Although I'd never played, my kind tended to take to new games easily. Fallon wouldn't know that though. Krakens were mythical creatures even among mythical creatures.

"Hmm, maybe it's the tentacles or something." My grin widened as one of the thick tendrils in question uncoiled from where it was wrapped around my forearm and gave Fallon a playful wave.

He shook his head and trotted over to me. "I've had enough getting my ass kicked for one day. Let's grab a drink and mingle."

Initially, I'd been hesitant to attend the party, but Atlas and Fallon were both adamant that I should be present.

I knew my appearance could be unsettling to humans and I hated the thought of any of Atlas and Tegan's guests feeling uncomfortable. It wasn't every day that you saw an ancient blue-green sea creature shuffling around on six tentacles. I resembled something you'd see in a Guillermo Del Toro film, not a guest at a backyard barbecue.

But that's what was refreshing about Briar Glenn. For the most part, the town and its inhabitants were supportive of the monster integration.

Fallon led the way to the cooler and I scuttled close behind him, my tentacles rolling and writhing over the grass to propel me along.

"Water for you, Cy?" he asked, digging through the cooler with his scaled talons.

"Please," I said, scanning the crowd around us. It was an interesting variety of humans and monsters, with the two groups intermixing and engaging in friendly conversation.

Fallon used his claw to pop the cap off his beer and just as he was about to speak, Atlas called out to us.

"Hey, guys. Come here for a second. I want you to meet Tegan's brother." The wolven shifted his giant body, and that's when I caught my first glimpse of *him*.

The rays from the sun caught his hair, illuminating the light red strands in a fiery blaze of color. His face was handsome—chiseled and masculine—with a thick mustache above his lip and a beard covering his jaw. A light dusting of freckles coated the bridge of his nose and cheeks. Forest green eyes accented with tiny flecks of gold assessed me, watching my every move as Fallon and I neared the small group.

As I came to a stop next to Atlas, the wolven affectionately placed a heavy paw on my shoulder. "This is Reece. He's the head of the parks department here in Briar Glenn." Atlas gave my shoulder a soft squeeze and smiled down at me.

I wasn't a small male, but it certainly felt that way when I stood next to Atlas.

Fallon cocked a talon in Reece's direction and ruffled his feathers. "Fallon. Nice to meet you, bud."

Reece paid him no attention and instead kept his vibrant green eyes focused on me.

This was exactly what I was afraid of.

I was a tentacled beast of the sea making the brother of my best friend's mate uncomfortable.

"Hello," I muttered. "I'm Cyrus. Cyrus Jennings." I extended a hand to Reece, my tentacle gripping my arm tightly, almost cutting off my circulation.

Reece stared at my outstretched palm for a moment, his handsome face set in a wary scowl.

It was like he was judging it.

Judging me.

Right when I was about to pull away and die from embarrassment, Reece placed his hand in mine.

His skin was soft and warm and as we shook he locked eyes with me. "Pleasure," he said in a baritone voice that had warmth spreading throughout my body.

As he spoke, it felt as if everything in the background became muted and faded away. For a moment that seemed to stretch on forever, it was Reece and I shaking hands, staring into one another's eyes.

But then it was over.

Reece cleared his throat before pulling his hand away and wiping it on the fabric of his khaki shorts.

His reaction surprised me. I wasn't wet and slimy like

an octopus. My skin and tentacles were smooth and cool to the touch, but they didn't leave behind any residue whatsoever.

Maybe his palm was sweaty?

A small frown tugged at the corner of my lips.

Atlas must have noticed and attempted to break some of the tension. "Reece is training for the Briar Glenn triathlon. He needs to work on his swim time, so we'll be seeing him at the gym." Atlas clapped the human on the back and Reece had to brace himself to avoid stumbling forward, obviously caught off-guard.

"Yeah, about that..." Reece started to say before Atlas cut him off.

"None of that. We're family now. The pool is there, use it. You'll probably see Cyrus there from time to time too."

Gods, Atlas could be oblivious sometimes. The fact that I utilized the pool probably wasn't a selling point for Reece.

"Uh, yeah. I use the pool quite a bit." My tentacles clenched tighter around my forearms with each word that came out of my mouth. One conversation with an attractive man and I was a ball of nerves.

"Hey, Atlas!" Tegan yelled. A raging inferno was coming from the grill in front of her. "Can you and Fallon give me a hand with this?"

"Holy shit," Fallon chirped. He and Atlas bolted to help her, leaving Reece and me standing alone.

He chuckled awkwardly as we watched the two monsters get the fire under control. "My sister was never much of a cook. Apparently, all her food-related skills went to baking. Thank gods Atlas seems to know his way around the kitchen or she'd still be eating out four times a week."

My mouth hung open in disbelief. "Four nights a week? Really?"

Again he laughed, but this time it was warmer, more genuine—like he was finally starting to relax in my presence. "Oh yeah, like a fucking teenager. Freaking teenager, sorry." He scrubbed a hand through that gorgeous red hair and bit his lip before turning away.

"No need to be sorry. There are actually studies that show people who swear are more intelligent." I gave him a thoughtful smile, admiring the way his expression brightened over my words.

"No shit?" he said with a laugh.

I chuckled, the soft fins along my neck flapping as my body vibrated.

They caught Reece's attention and he cleared his throat, the jovial nature of our conversation ending right then and there.

My tentacles shuffled beneath me. I needed to think of something to fill the uncomfortable lull in conversation.

"So, uh, you work for the parks department, right?" *Stick to your guns, Cyrus. Go with what you know.*

"Yup," Reece said, his full lower lip popping the P.

"That must be an interesting job."

He shrugged and his muscular shoulders strained against the fabric of his shirt. "It's alright. We maintain the baseball fields and keep the parks clean. I get to spend most of my time outside, so I can't complain. If you don't mind me asking, uh—" He lowered his voice and whispered, "What are you?"

"Oh, I'm an artist. Oil paintings mostly but—"

He cut me off and stepped closer. "No, I meant what kind of monster are you? I've never seen another monster like you before. And ya know, your accent. You're obviously from another country."

I tried not to be angry or offended. Reece was a human.

Curiosity was in their nature. But there was a part of me that strongly disliked explaining exactly what I was and all of the little idiosyncrasies that came along with it.

"Well, I'm a kraken. And as for my accent, I spent the majority of my life in a seaside town on the coast of England. It's likely you've never seen one of my kind before because there aren't many of us left."

All of the color seemed to drain from his face and his thick mustache pursed down over his lip. "Shit. I'm sorry. I fucking knew that was a stupid question."

As if by its own accord, one of my tentacles unraveled and snaked around his forearm. It was one of my breeding tentacles, my hectocotylus, and the moment it made contact with his skin—*I almost came.*

Oh, gods no.

That was a male kraken's mate bond response.

There was no way that this was happening.

The three hearts inside of my chest thumped rapidly, and I fought to get my words out, to do anything to hide the fact that Reece Rollins and I were mates.

I tried to play it cool but blurted out the words in one breath. "I-It's fine. Really. It's normal to be curious about things that are different from us. Especially for humans."

Reece looked down at where we were attached before wrenching his arm away. He stared at where the frond had gripped him with a panicked expression.

"I gotta get going," he mumbled under his breath before stalking off, presumably to say goodbye to Atlas and Tegan.

As I watched him walk away from me, it felt as if I'd been punched in the gut. Of course a man like him would find a monster like me repulsive. And of course, out of all the beings I'd met in my long life, that man was my mate.

FOUR

Reece

"Motherfucker!" I yelled the minute I slammed my front door shut.

What in the ever-loving fuck was wrong with me?

For the most part, I'd managed to keep my cool while surrounded by monsters at the party, but there was something about Cyrus that unsettled me.

There were so many reasons why too.

The fact that he didn't wear clothes, his pointed head and fins, and *those tentacles.*

I tried my best to be polite, but when he reached out and touched me, I couldn't help but pull away. It was hard enough for me to accept affection from the people I loved, but a strange monster I just met?

Hard no.

I really hoped he wouldn't tell Atlas or Tegan what happened. Until that moment, everything had gone so well. We were all getting along and then I had to go and do something to fuck it up.

Why did he have to touch me?

And why the fuck did I have to react that way?

"Shit." I huffed under my breath and threw myself down onto the couch.

My head whirled with thoughts of the party and I replayed the interaction between Cyrus and me on a loop.

Gods, I needed to expend some energy and clear my thoughts.

I got all my gear on, rolled my bike out from where I kept it in the garage, and pedaled off toward the lake.

Dusk was settling over Briar Glenn, so I turned on my bike lamp to illuminate the winding back roads in front of me.

I was such a fucking idiot.

I wondered if what Cyrus said was true. About people who curse being more intelligent. I mean, I wasn't a rocket scientist, but I'd always done well in school. I excelled at pretty much anything I put my mind to.

Since childhood, it was always drilled into my head that I had to be the best. I was pushed to be the fastest and the strongest.

Ultimately, us humans were no match for monsters.

They were wildly superior.

Atlas could kill me in a second, and I was sure that Cyrus would destroy me in trivia *and* in the pool.

Krakens.

Why weren't there more of his kind?

I could have asked if I hadn't completely offended him.

What in the actual fuck was that?

Why couldn't I be normal about a little friendly gesture?

So what if he was a monster?

All he did was touch my arm with his tentacle. It wasn't like he smacked my ass with it or something.

Sweat dripped down my face as I pulled my bike to a stop in front of the lake.

The sun was setting, reflecting its bright red rays off of the lake's surface, almost like it was on fire.

In a few short months, I'd be jumping into that cold water and swimming like my life depended on it, and I was wildly unprepared.

I needed to get my ass in gear and get in the pool.

Atlas wouldn't have offered to let me train at Leviathan if he didn't mean it. It wasn't like my sister put him up to that shit.

But swimming at Leviathan meant that I'd run into Cyrus at some point.

And when I did, I'd have to apologize for my behavior at the party.

I saw the hurt flash over his face at my reaction, but in the moment I was too much of a prick to care.

Monsters were a part of life here in Briar Glenn, and they weren't going away.

I had to get over this fear.

I unhooked my phone from where I had it clipped to my handlebars and typed out a text to my baby sister.

Hey Teg. Had a great time at the party. Can you ask Atlas when I should stop by Leviathan and see him about swimming there?

I puffed out a breath and hit send. My sister would probably see this as me being selfish and taking advantage of her mate—and in a way it was—but it would also give me an opportunity to chat with Atlas some more. And even Fallon, although the griffon gave off major gym bro vibes.

These monsters were important to her, though. Therefore, they had to be important to me.

My phone buzzed with a notification.

Tegan: We were really glad you came, and I know Mom was too. Atlas said to stop by next Wednesday and he'll get you signed up. Have a good night, Reecie!

Reecie.

That was what Tegan called me when we were kids. Shit, it had been years since she'd referred to me as Reecie.

It was my fault that things were like this between us. I'd been such a stubborn, insufferable ass about the whole monster integration, about Atlas, about a lot of things really.

I was so tired of letting my past and my fears dictate my life.

It was time for me to work on moving forward.

FIVE

Cyrus

"Somefin' is boverin' you," Fallon slurred from where he was sprawled out in the backseat of my SUV. It was preplanned that I would be his designated driver, but I hadn't anticipated him drinking quite this much.

"Nothing is bothering me."

I kept my eyes on the road and tightened my grip on the steering wheel. I really didn't need him blabbing to Atlas about what happened. Tegan would inevitably find out and it would get back to Reece that I'd said something... And the mating bond? There was no way I was even remotely ready to talk about that. I was still processing it myself.

Fallon sat up and leaned in close, "I know you, Cyyyy... Did somefin' happen with Reece?"

Gods. We'd been friends for too long. He knew something was up. Just like he always did.

I took a deep breath, and the tentacles wrapped around my arms relaxed slightly. "I—I think I made Tegan's brother uncomfortable. We were talking and my tentacle reached out and grabbed his arm."

"Tha' doesn't sound too bad. You're a touchy-feely kinna' guy."

I sighed and rubbed the fin on the side of my head with one of my tentacles. Fallon could be exhausting, especially when he was drunk.

"He pulled his arm away so fast." I lowered my voice. "Like he thought I was disgusting."

Fallon gasped so loud I nearly swerved the car into oncoming traffic.

"Fallon!" I yelled, but he was completely unaffected.

The griffon simply leaned closer and nuzzled his beak against my shoulder. "Don't you ever say tha', Cy. You're beautiful. Tha' guy is an asshole."

I tried to fight off a smile. Even if he was annoying and drunk, Fallon was a good friend. And he was right, Reece was an asshole. A handsome asshole, but still an asshole.

"Thanks, Fal." I ran a tentacle through the downy feathers along his neck.

"Do you thin' we can stop at Tito's Tacos on the way home? I'm starving."

I sighed again. *Exhausting.* "Sure."

After getting Tito's Tacos, helping Fallon into our apartment and to the bathroom so he could throw up Tito's Tacos, I made sure he got into his room safely, then collapsed onto my bed.

I stared up at the stars through my skylight as the light of the moon drifted down into my room.

Every time I closed my eyes and tried to drift off to sleep, the same image clouded my brain: Reece Rollins.

As Fallon and I had already established, the guy was an asshole. But he was hot. There was something about my mate that called to the creative part of my brain.

For the first time in months, I felt inspired.

I had to paint him.

The apartment was fairly quiet as I shuffled across the hall to my studio. Light snores came from Fallon's room, but he wouldn't be waking anytime soon. Even if he did, he was used to my odd hours. He'd probably feel relieved that I was painting again.

My tentacle flicked the light switch, illuminating the open space with warm, white light. For me, this room was the major draw of the apartment.

One wall was composed entirely of windows, allowing an abundance of natural light to fill the studio during the day, and the black of the starlit sky to shroud the space at night.

The opposite wall was lined with canvases. Some were finished pieces awaiting gallery display and others were pristine white backdrops, ready for inspiration to strike.

And tonight it had in the form of a fiery-haired god.

I queued up The Cure on my phone and Robert Smith's crooning voice flowed out of the studio's surround sound, allowing me to get lost in the music while I set to work sketching out the scene.

For several hours, I painted, applying layer after layer of color to the canvas until the sun began to rise.

I hummed the notes in unison with the guitar, my head bobbing to the beat of the music with each stroke of my brush against the canvas.

My tentacle stilled as the last few notes drifted out of the speakers and I shuffled back to get a better look at the piece I was working on.

I'd covered the canvas in a dusky, sea blue color. In the center, I'd painted a merman and a human man tangled together in a romantic embrace. Sunlight filtered down into the water, illuminating the bright red strands of the human man's hair—almost like a halo.

The merman's handsome face was solemn as he clung to his lover beneath the surface. He knew their time together was waning. Two worlds separated by vast differences.

It was wishful thinking.

All the things I'd dreamt of laid out on canvas.

Would my mate ever look at me that way?

I'd never be a handsome merman.

With a deep sigh, I rinsed my brushes, shut off the lights, and closed the door to the studio.

SIX

Reece

The soles of my slides slapped along the pavement as I walked up to the front door of Leviathan Fitness. I wiped my clammy hands on my shorts before reaching for the door handle.

Why the fuck was I so nervous?

Oh, right. Because I was walking into a gym full of monsters.

Atlas stood behind the front desk and gave me a friendly wave as I walked through the door.

"Hey, man! How are you this morning?" He smiled, the sharp tips of his teeth showing. "Come on over and we'll get you all set up. Tegan is super excited you decided to join."

"I, uh, I appreciate you doing this for me. I really need to work on my swim."

Atlas slid some papers and a pen across the counter to me. "It's no problem at all. We're family."

I gave him a sincere smile.

What could I say? The wolven was growing on me.

I scribbled my signature on the forms and handed them back to Atlas.

"Welcome to Leviathan Fitness!" He grinned before turning around to dig through a cabinet. "What size shirt do you wear?"

"Uh, extra large, please."

He passed me a black T-shirt with the Leviathan Fitness logo in the corner.

The tentacle and the weight.

It all made sense now.

Cyrus was the inspiration behind the gym's logo.

The two of them had to be close.

Knowing that I'd upset one of Atlas's best friends made me feel like even more of an asshole.

Atlas was acting normal and I hadn't received any angry text messages from my sister, so I guessed Cyrus had kept our awkward interaction on the down low.

For the time being, I was in the clear.

Now if I could avoid running into him.

"Let me show you to the pool," Atlas said as he walked around the counter.

I slung the T-shirt over my shoulder and followed behind him, doing my best to keep up.

Gods, he was massive.

If his equipment matched the rest of him, how did he and my sister even work?

My face scrunched up at the thought.

Don't think about your sibling doing the deed.

Fucking gross.

"Here we are!" Atlas said as he pushed open a door labeled 'Pool'.

It opened to reveal a bright room with glass panels covering the ceiling, and a shimmering Olympic swimming pool smack dab in the center.

"Shit," I mumbled under my breath. "This is really nice."

Atlas let out a deep, rumbling laugh that roared through the open space. "Thank you. It's saltwater too. None of the smell or sting of chlorine. I wanted the gym to be state of the art."

He pointed with a clawed finger to an area labeled 'Locker Room'. "You'll find the showers in there." He looked down at his watch. "I have to get back to the desk, but after your swim, I'll give you the full tour. How's that sound?"

Movement in the water on the opposite end of the pool briefly caught my attention.

Shit.

"Oh yeah. Cyrus is here for a swim. If you have any questions about the facility, he should be able to help." Atlas gripped my shoulder affectionately, and I had to force myself not to shy away from his touch.

"Uh, sounds good. I'll catch up with you later about that tour," I said quietly, watching the blue-green kraken glide through the water.

He gave me a nod and headed back through the door.

I puffed out a breath and ran my fingers through my hair.

This was just my luck.

My first day using the pool, and of course, Cyrus was here, because why wouldn't he be.

Stepping into the locker room, I sat down on the bench in the middle of the aisle and rubbed my hand along my beard.

It wasn't like I could leave. I just got here. Atlas would think something was up. And I really did need to work on my swim time.

I mean, we'd be in the water. We'd both be focused on swimming.

It wasn't like there'd be a ton of time for idle chit-chat. If I stayed in my own swim lane, maybe he wouldn't even know I was there.

"Motherfucker," I grumbled as I pulled my t-shirt over my head and threw my shit in the locker.

Deep breaths, Reece.

Deep breaths.

He isn't going to drag you under or something.

I strolled out to the pool and stood by the ladder for a moment, my eyes scanning the water, looking for Cyrus.

The kraken was near the bottom of the pool, his tentacles undulating and propelling his body through the water with ease. He seemed to glide along fluidly, becoming one with the water around him. I was mesmerized, and for several minutes I stood there and watched him.

Not once did he come up to the surface to take a breath.

I would have been content to stand there and watch him forever, but I had to be at work in an hour and a half. I needed to get my ass in the water.

The metal of the ladder was cold on my feet as I lowered myself into the water. I hissed the moment my dick bobbed beneath the surface. It was chilly, but compared to the lake, it felt like bathwater.

I made a mental note to do more research on open water triathlon swimming and plunged underwater.

With my eyes closed, I focused on my technique, kicking my feet and using my arms to drag my body through the water. Swimming was the only time I found my muscular body to be a hindrance to my performance. I didn't have that lean swimmer's physique, and that made this so much harder.

My hair stuck to my face while I swam, making the periodic visual checks I should have been doing nearly impossible. Like a dumbass, I'd forgotten my swim cap and goggles.

I was almost to the opposite end of the pool when my body slammed into something solid.

FUCK.

Cyrus's voice.

I'd heard his voice in my head.

I splashed and sputtered, trying to tread water and catch my breath while being simultaneously terrified.

Cyrus stared at me, his wide blue eyes unblinking.

"Are you alright?" he asked in that fucking British accent.

"Yeah," I said, flipping my hair out of my eyes. "Are you?"

"I'm fine." He was floating in the water without issue, his tentacles open in a wide parachute below his waist.

Wild.

"Did you, uh, did you talk to me in my head? Was I imagining that?" The words rushed out with a light spray of salt water as I began to panic. "Can you read my mind?" I blurted out.

Cyrus stared at me for several beats, his eyes unblinking and his mouth a thin line—but then the corners of his lips turned up slightly and his fins began to vibrate with laughter.

Heat spread over my cheeks and I slapped the water, splashing Cyrus in the face. "You fucker."

Beads of water rolled off his slick skin as he smiled, revealing sharp teeth that looked like something you'd see on a piranha.

It was slightly terrifying, but I did my best to stay calm.

"I can't read your mind. But I can communicate with

you using *my* mind. Telepathy," he said. "It's theorized that my kind evolved the trait in order to communicate underwater. It also comes in handy when I'm trying to let Fallon know I'm ready to leave the bar."

I tilted my head in confusion. "Are the two of you, like, a couple or something?"

Cyrus barked with laughter as if it was the funniest thing he'd ever heard.

"Ah, shit, mate. That's hilarious." He sighed and caught his breath. "We're roommates. Not lovers. I'm into males, but he isn't my type."

I bit my lip and nodded my head.

So Cyrus was gay too.

An uncomfortable silence stretched out between us. I wasn't sure if I should mention what happened at the party and apologize for my behavior, or pretend like it never happened and not bring it up.

"So, uh, how is training going? I see you forgot your goggles." He raised the bumpy protrusions above his eyes that I assumed were a kraken's version of eyebrows.

"Yeah, and my swim cap. So I'd say it isn't going well."

"I saw you watching me," he said with a smirk.

Fuck.

I might as well fess up to it.

"I mean, I was. You make it look so easy. And it must be when you're built for swimming. I drag ass through the water."

"I was watching you for a bit before you ran into me." He looked away from me and smiled. "You're a shit swimmer," he mumbled under his breath.

I grunted and swam over to the side of the pool, crossing my arms over the edge. Treading water while we talked was exhausting.

Cyrus swam up beside me and used his tentacles to haul his body out of the water with ease. I was in awe as I watched them ripple and writhe in a swirling mass of blues and greens. His coloring reminded me of a raging sea, which made sense for a kraken, I guess. It really was pretty.

He positioned himself so he was sitting on the ledge, his tentacles dangling into the water.

"I may not be an expert, but I could train you, you know. Help with some of your mechanics. If you'd take the help, that is."

I looked up at his alien-like face, his fins lightly flapping, and those unblinking eyes. "You'd do that? Even after what happened at the party?"

He dipped his head. "I'm sorry. For touching you without your permission. Sometimes my tentacles have a mind of their own."

I couldn't believe what I was hearing.

He was apologizing to me?

When I was the one who acted like a complete and utter dick to him?

"No, I'm sorry. I shouldn't have acted that way." I lowered my voice, even though it was only the two of us in the pool. "Sometimes I'm weird about touch and, like, affectionate gestures."

Cyrus raised his head and stared at me. "I heard from Fallon that you don't like monsters."

Fucking Fallon and his big fucking mouth.

"Monsters make me a little uneasy. You're just—different." I gestured to his tentacles as they languidly swayed in the water. "But I'm trying. And if the offer still stands, I could really use some help in the swimming department." I sighed and squinted up at Cyrus as saltwater dripped down my forehead and into my eyes.

A wide grin spread over his face. With those sharp teeth, it was almost menacing—*almost*. "Well, Reece Rollins, you've got yourself a swim coach."

SEVEN

Cyrus

"Cyrus, are you out of your mind?" Fallon squawked from where he sat at the kitchen island.

As usual, I was preparing lunch and he was sitting on his ass watching me, expecting the food to just appear in front of him.

"This is Reece we're talking about. Tegan's asshole brother Reece. He gives you one weak-ass apology about his behavior at the party and you just forgive him?" Fallon cocked his head from side to side and wiggled his talons. "Oh, Reece. It's fine. I forgive you. I'll train you." He mocked in a gods-awful British accent.

"First of all, that is a terrible impression of me—"

"I thought it was pretty good," he said under his breath.

"Second of all, he said he's trying. His sister is marrying our best friend. I'm simply—" I turned around to face him and held my arms out. "Trying to extend an olive branch of sorts."

"I'm telling you, man. This is a bad idea." He let out a long whistle and bristled his feathers.

I whipped back around and continued to aggressively chop the vegetables for our stir fry.

Fallon's reaction to the news made total sense, given his understanding of the situation between Reece and me. But there was no way I was ready to reveal the fact that he was my mate. I was still coming to terms with it myself.

And if the news got back to Reece?

It would be disastrous.

He was just now starting to warm up to monsters.

Having that bomb dropped on him when he least expected it?

I was positive it would lead to instant rejection.

There was nothing in the world worse than being rejected by your mate. It was likely I wouldn't survive it.

And, to be honest, I wasn't sure I would want to.

Coaching Reece would give him an opportunity to get to know me better, and perhaps with time, he would develop feelings for me.

But maybe that was wishful thinking.

I spun the wok with my hand while my tentacle used a wooden spoon to stir the dish, focusing all of my attention on the stir-fry instead of debating with Fallon.

"Cyrus," he said from behind me. "I worry about you. That's all. You've been going through it lately."

I stilled and my fins perked up.

Other than not painting, I'd thought I was acting normal. Had it really been that obvious that I was struggling?

I didn't give Fallon enough credit. He could be tiring, but he was a good friend.

I plated our food, setting a bowl in front of him before taking a seat beside him at the island.

"Thank you." Fallon clicked his beak with excitement.

"You're welcome. It's hot."

I shook my head as the impatient griffon brought a forkful of stir fry up to his beak.

"I know you worry, but I'm a grown man, Fallon. One that is centuries older than you are, in fact. I've just lost my way a bit. It feels like everyone else around me is growing and changing, and I'm stuck in the same place."

"Even though you're older than me, I'm still allowed to be concerned about you. I mean, I get it. Being single as fuck and watching our buddy meet someone and fall in love quickly. It sucks."

I laughed around a mouthful of food. "Fallon Ridgewing, Briar Glenn's biggest player, is lamenting about being single? I never thought I'd see the day." My tentacle reached out and nudged his shoulder.

He shrugged, his talons making the gesture look ridiculous. "What can I say? Summer will be over before we know it and then it's cuffing season."

I stared at him, tilting my head in confusion. *These kids and their slang.* "What in the goddess's name is 'cuffing season'?"

Fallon let out a chirpy laugh and fluttered his wings slightly. "Cuffing season is basically the fall and winter. The cold months when people don't want to be single and jump into relationships."

"But why cuffing?"

"You know, like handcuffed. Being tied down."

I nodded my head in understanding. That made sense. Maybe I'd have someone of my own to warm my bed this cuffing season.

Gods, I was getting ahead of myself.

"Shit," Fallon mumbled with a noodle dangling from his beak. "I gotta get going or I'm gonna be late for work." He bolted off of his barstool and grabbed his pre-workout drink from the fridge. "So when's your first training session with him?"

"Monday. We'll be training a few days a week."

Fallon clipped his bag around his neck and tilted his head in my direction. "*Diving* right into it I see."

I rolled my eyes and he warbled with laughter. Gods, he was such an idiot.

"I had to," he said after he caught his breath. "Thanks for lunch, bud. I'll see ya later."

Fallon opened the front door, yelling over his shoulder, "And get some painting done! I can't afford the rent by myself!"

Cheeky fucker.

He was well aware I had enough money stockpiled for *multiple* lifetimes, but he loved to tease and play up the whole "starving artist" thing.

Fallon was right, though, I did need to do some painting. And thanks to my new muse, my well of creativity was practically overflowing.

After cleaning the kitchen, I shuffled down the hall to my studio. The windowed room was warm and brightly lit by the light of the afternoon sun.

It was perfect for what I wanted to paint.

The *only* thing I wanted to paint.

I grabbed a pencil and pulled my stool in front of one of the blank canvases lining the wall. I closed my eyes and thought back to how Reece looked as he stared up at me from the ledge of the pool: those emerald eyes shimmering bright, the freckles dotting his muscular forearms, and the way the water dripped off his beard down into the pool.

Despite the fact that I'd been around for a long time, I wasn't always certain of *everything*, but I was certain that

Reece Rollins was one of the prettiest men I had ever seen.

With his machismo exterior, he probably wouldn't want to hear that, but it was the truth. You could be masculine and pretty. They weren't mutually exclusive.

As I finished the final line of my sketch, my phone buzzed from where it sat on the cart that held my paints.

My tentacles clenched tight to my arms, almost forcing me to drop my phone.

I couldn't believe what I was seeing.

It was like he knew he was on my mind.

Unknown: Hey Cyrus. It's Reece. I got your number from Atlas. Are you available to meet a little later in the morning for training Monday? Around 10 am?

Reece Rollins.

My mate.

Had asked for my phone number.

The other morning at the gym was such a whirlwind that I'd completely forgotten to exchange our contact info.

I saved his number in my phone, then typed out a response.

Cyrus: Hello! 10 a.m. works for me.

I hesitated before hitting send.

Should I add have a nice night?

See you Monday?

Shit.

Even if Fallon was home, it wasn't like I could ask him for advice on this. It would be a dead giveaway that I had some sort of interest in Reece. See you Monday was probably my best bet.

Cyrus: Hello! 10 a.m. works for me. See you Monday.

I hit send and stared at my phone, still in shock that somewhere in Briar Glenn, Reece was choosing me of all people to message.

His response was almost immediate.

Reece: See you then. Have a nice night!

I smiled at my phone before sitting it back down on my supply cart.

It would be a nice night.

Because tonight, I was going to paint another portrait of the most beautiful man I had ever seen, and next week, I'd get to spend time with him.

Sure, I'd be giving him the adult, triathlon version of swim lessons, but it was still time with him.

Time with my mate.

As I started to mix my color palette for tonight's painting, the merman portrait from the other day caught my eye.

It really was a gorgeous piece. Gallery worthy, even.

One of my tentacles snatched my phone from the cart and I rang up Eduardo.

He answered on the first ring.

"Cyrus, I've been worried about you. I thought you might be dead." He huffed.

"Nope, very much alive. I've been in a bit of a slump—but I think that's over now. Can I send you some photos of my recent work? I think I want to put on a show."

Eduardo screamed with excitement, and I smiled.

I was back.

EIGHT

Reece

Tucking my phone into my pocket, I smiled. It was cool that Cyrus was flexible, considering he was the one doing me a favor.

"What's got you smiling?" Jimenez asked as he opened the passenger door of our work truck and passed me a cup of coffee.

"Nothing. Uh, just in a good mood today, that's all." I took a sip of my coffee and started the truck, hoping that he didn't press me on the subject.

"Are you sure you don't mind covering for me on Sunday? I know it's sort of last minute—"

"Nah. It's cool. Cyrus said he'd meet me at the pool around ten on Monday, so it works out."

"You know, I've seen him around town. He's not too bad looking." Jimenez took a swig of his coffee and raised his perfectly shaped brows.

"Is this really happening right now? You're telling me you find Cyrus attractive?"

He shrugged and looked out the window. "I don't know. It's something about the tentacles. I saw this anime once—"

I slammed on the brakes, almost sending coffee flying all over the interior of the truck.

"Stop it. Stop it right now. I don't want to hear about any freaky cartoon porn or how you think that Cyrus is hot."

Jimenez looked over and flashed me a shit-eating grin. "I didn't say he was hot. That was all you, boss."

"Jimenez! I did not!" I barked.

I didn't think Cyrus was hot, and I didn't need my employee busting my balls about it.

I stomped on the gas, sending the truck speeding down the road toward the park, while Jimenez busted out laughing.

"Chill! I was just playing around. You're gonna get us pulled over," he said and cackled even louder.

"Fuck off," I grumbled under my breath.

I pulled into our usual spot, adjacent to the athletic fields, and got out of the truck.

"Hey, I'm sorry. I know you're sensitive about the whole monster thing." Jimenez walked around to where I was leaning against the truck.

"It's been a lot. The integration, the shit with my sister, what happened with Cyrus at the party."

Jimenez gave me a thoughtful smile and leaned against the truck beside me. "Well, the integration has gone great. Briar Glenn is the same sleepy town it was before. And the stuff with Tegan, it's getting better. I know the two of you used to be close. She probably misses that just as much as you do."

"You're right, but I was still a total dickhead to Cyrus at the party."

"You apologized and he forgave your ass, right? Plus, he agreed to coach you. It seems like he's trying to move past it, and you should too. But if it's really bothering you, you could do something nice for him to show your appreciation and work towards making amends."

"Like what?"

"I don't know. Maybe take him to lunch or something after training. Get to know the guy a little bit. He *is* one of Atlas's best friends. You're gonna be spending a lot of time together over the next few months, might as well make the best of it."

Sipping my coffee, I nodded my head.

Cyrus and I would be spending a lot of time together. Time that he wasn't being compensated for in any way. The least I could do was take him out to lunch a time or two.

What kind of food did he like?

Calamari was probably out of the question.

I chuckled at my own joke, and looked over at Jimenez, wondering if he'd heard me. His deep brown eyes were fixed on the centaur couple playing frisbee in the field like they did every afternoon.

"You wanna join them for a game, Jimenez?"

"Nah." He laughed and shook his head. "They're just nice to look at."

"Would you date a monster?"

Jimenez smoothed his thumb over his lower lip, nodding his head slightly before fixing his brown eyes on me. "Yeah, I think I would."

I snapped my mouth open to protest, but shut it just as fast. I was curious about what he had to say. Sure, Jimenez was young, but he was also pretty wise.

"Boss. Reece. Times are changing. And I mean no disrespect, but you're gonna need to change too. Monsters are a part of our world now. They're not bloodthirsty killers, or here to run us out of town." He took another sip of his coffee. "Gods, Reece. Your sister is marrying a monster. You see how happy they are. You're telling me that if a monster brought you that kind of happiness you'd push them away?" He shook his head. "You'd have to be out of your gods damn mind not to want what they have. Man or monster, who gives a fuck. Love is love."

I stood there for a moment, quietly contemplating what Jimenez said. The mayor's daughter and the satyr, Atlas and Tegan. Every day there were more human and monster relationships popping up in Briar Glenn.

Everyone around me was opening their lives and their hearts to monsters. Meanwhile, I was the same miserable prick I'd always been, with nothing to show for it.

"Gods dammit, Jimenez. Why do you have to be so fucking smart?" I huffed, crossing my arms over my chest.

He shrugged his shoulders and smiled. "It's both a blessing and a curse. Someone's gotta call you out on your shit."

Even if I didn't say it, I was thankful that he did.

NINE

Cyrus

"Hey, buddy!" Atlas greeted me with a smile as I shuffled through the doors of Leviathan. He leaned across the front desk and waved me over to him.

"Chai feeling sick again?" I asked.

Frowning, Atlas nodded his head in confirmation.

Chai, a minotaur, was one of the trainers at the gym, and recently she'd been missing a lot of time due to some mysterious illness. Atlas had taken to covering the front desk in her absence, though a wolven greeting you with a sharp-toothed smile the moment you walked through the door had a bit of a different effect.

"Gods damn. Poor thing can't catch a break."

"Yeah, she's going through it. I think Tegan and I are gonna swing by her house and check on her later this week. Are you training Reece today?"

"Indeed, I am. He's meeting me here at ten." My tentacle unraveled from my arm and pulled on the bright red whistle hanging from my neck. "I even got this bad boy. Wanted to be professional, you know."

Atlas chuckled and shook his head. "Oh, man. I'm sure

Reece is going to love that. You better watch yourself with that one, Cy."

My tentacles clenched tight to my forearms. *Oh, I'd watch myself with Reece, alright.*

It was an innocent enough comment, but the fact that he was my mate had my mind reeling with all sorts of possibilities.

"Cyrus? You alright?" Atlas leaned in closer, his head tilted and his bright yellow eyes searching my face.

Oh yeah, Atlas. Just having sexual fantasies about your soon-to-be brother-in-law. No biggie.

I cleared my throat awkwardly and shrugged my shoulders. "I'm fine. I'm, uh, just a little tired. Fallon got in late last night and woke me up."

Not a huge stretch from the truth. Fallon did get in late last night after sampling his current flavor of the week. So much for cuffing season...

"Okay well, you know I'm here for you if you ever need to talk, right?"

Gods, my friends were the best, but this concern over my mental state working its way into every single conversation needed to end.

"Right. Right. I'm aware. And, uh, I meant to tell you, and Fallon too, that I've been painting again. I rang Eduardo about a gallery show the other day."

Atlas flashed me a wide grin, the pointed tips of his teeth peeking out from beneath his lip. "Right on, bud!" He reached across the counter and shook my shoulder. "I knew you'd shake that painter's block. Do you have a theme for the show?"

"Not yet. It's kind of a hodgepodge right now, but I think I'll be able to tie it all together."

Realization dawned on me.

What in the goddess's name had I done?

I was going to exhibit a gallery full of paintings of Reece Rollins and hope that no one noticed?

I'd already sent Eduardo photos of my current pieces. There was no way he'd let me back out now.

Besides, the gallery wasn't *in* Briar Glenn—the town was much too small for that. And it wasn't like my friends came to all of my shows anyway.

It would be fine.

Everything would be fine.

I was getting myself worked up over nothing.

I'd handle it when the time came. For now, I had more pressing matters. Like molding Reece Rollins into an Olympic swimmer.

"Well, I should probably head over to the pool. I want to do a few laps to recharge before Reece gets here. Say hello to the missus for me, will you?"

At that, Atlas smiled and his body swayed with the wagging of his tail. "Will do. And Cy, good luck. You know where to find me if you need me."

My tentacle gave him a little wave, and I shuffled off down the corridor that led to the pool.

As usual, the pool room was empty. I could count on my tentacles the number of times I'd run into other swimmers here, but that's what made it the ideal place to train Reece.

I'd also heard from Fallon that it was the ideal place for *other things* too. Gods damn voyeur.

I fixed my wide eyes on the clock.

It was only nine-thirty, so I had plenty of time for a swim before Reece arrived. Even though I'd be in the water for some of his drills, I planned to spend the majority of the session on the pool deck, monitoring his form. From what

I'd seen the last time we were in the pool together, we had a lot to work on.

I scuttled to the edge of the pool as fast as I could before diving in, the water gliding over my body and barely making a splash. The lengths of my tentacles undulated, opening the thin skin that connected them like a parachute, propelling me through the water like a torpedo.

As the saltwater absorbed into my skin, my body hummed with pleasure.

The pool wasn't the churning depths of the open ocean, but it was still a comfort, one I was thankful for each time my body needed a little pick me up.

I swam the length of the pool, twisting and twirling in the water until my three hearts were pounding. I drifted to the bottom, lying on my back and blinking up at where the sunlight filtered down through the water while my heart rates slowed.

My mind drifted back to my mate. All I could think about lately was Reece.

Gods, he had looked breathtaking emerging from the pool. Water trickled down his body and collected in the fluffy happy trail that disappeared beneath his swim trunks.

I wanted to trail my tentacle over it before sliding it down his shorts, wrapping it around the stiff length of his cock and giving it harsh strokes.

It had been so long since I'd been intimate with someone.

Sure, I'd had partners. Tentacles were actually quite popular amongst humans, but I'd never felt that *connection*.

If you had told me centuries ago that a monster-wary human would be my mate, I would have laughed.

But here we were.

I noticed a shadowy figure staring down at me from the edge of the pool.

Reece was here for our training session.

I shot toward the surface, giving him a wide smile the moment my head crested out of the water.

"Gods damn. You're impressive in the water." He shook his head and the corner of his lips turned up in a slight smile.

To most people, it probably wouldn't seem like that big of a compliment. I was a kraken, after all. But hearing it from Reece. Hearing it from my mate...

You would have thought he hung the stars and named one after me.

"Thank you." I let out a shy laugh and hauled myself out of the water with my tentacles. Reece stood next to where I sat on the edge of the pool and I stared up at him. "I watched a bunch of videos about swimming techniques last night and I have some ideas on how we can improve your form."

What I really meant was I was up until three A.M. watching swimming instructional videos for triathletes in preparation for this, but he didn't need all the details.

Reece scrubbed a hand through his beard and looked down at me. "I, uh, I really do appreciate this, Cyrus."

"It's no problem. Truly. Why don't you get changed and we'll get started."

He nodded his head, then walked off toward the locker room.

Again, I was hit with disbelief. Reece Rollins was my mate, and today we would be spending time together. Alone.

Gods, he'd looked so good too. But not nearly as good as

he did when he emerged from the locker room a few minutes later.

Reece walked over to me in his swim trunks, his well-toned abs tapering to that happy trail.

"Do you have your swim cap and goggles this time?" I teased and slid the whistle back and forth along my neck nervously.

"Yes, coach," he responded with a wry smile curling his lips. Pulling the cap out of his pocket, he slipped it onto his head before putting on his goggles. "Look okay?" he asked as he tucked a few stray strands of light orange hair into the cap.

"You look great, but um, what's with the trunks?"

Reece looked down, tugging at the loose material of his trunks. "What about them?"

"Well, you already have a lot of drag because of your muscles. If we can eliminate any additional drag, you'll swim faster. So you know, wearing trunks that are a little more fitted is great for reducing drag."

He put his hands on his hips and bit his lip. "So, like a banana hammock? I really don't want my junk hanging out there."

My laughter echoed out through the room. While I'd enjoy seeing it, that wasn't exactly what I had in mind. "Gods, no. They make something called jammers. They're essentially compression shorts you can swim in."

"Thank gods. I have a tri suit, but I can't really use that for pool training. I'll order myself some jammers after we finish up." He shifted his weight from leg to leg. "Um, speaking of, when we're done training, I was wondering if you wanted to get lunch together. Ya know, as a thank you."

Had my mate just asked me out?

I mean, technically, it was a platonic lunch date. But the

fact that he asked and that we'd be spending time together outside of training was enough to make my hearts flutter.

I couldn't help the wide smile that spread over my face. "That would be very nice, thank you. Did you have somewhere in mind?"

He pursed his lips, his mustache curling down over his mouth. It was adorable. Like a grumpy walrus. "My first thought was sushi because I'm on a meal plan right now, but I wasn't sure if—"

My fins flapped as I laughed. "Reece. I'm a sea creature. Fish eat other fish all the time. Sushi is perfect."

His face turned pink as he rubbed his hand over the back of his neck. "Sushi it is, then. What are we doing today?"

Reece fixed his gaze on my whistle, the bright green of his irises intensified by his goggles.

"I was thinking I'd have you do a few laps back and forth, get a better sense of your form, then we'd work on corrections and move to a few drills. On top of my understanding of swimming mechanics, I did some research last night. How long do we have before the triathlon?"

"Well, it's July now, so that gives us about three months." His expression dropped slightly.

It was obvious he was nervous about this part of the race and doubted his abilities, but I was determined to help him.

"Hey," I said, stepping closer to him. I had to remind myself not to touch him, even though my instincts as his mate were riding me to comfort him. "We have plenty of time. We're going to get you where you need to be. You've got this."

He nodded and I gave him a reassuring smile before moving toward the edge of the pool.

I brought the whistle up to my lips and gave it two harsh

blows, the shrill sound bouncing off the walls of the open room.

"Fuck," Reece whispered under his breath and clenched his jaw.

"What are you doing just standing there?" I asked. "Get your ass in the pool."

Gods, I could already tell I was going to love this.

TEN

Reece

For the next two hours, Cyrus sat on the edge of the pool and gently criticized me for how much of a shit swimmer I was.

And that whistle. *That fucking whistle.*

There was a part of me that wanted to shove it down his throat, but there was another part of me that appreciated how seriously he was taking this.

I mean, Cyrus had done his research on triathlon swimming drills, as well as the appropriate training gear.

Plus, his advice was actually *helpful*.

Sure, my body hurt like hell, but I could already tell that with his modifications to my form I was improving.

"Great job today, Reece," he said as I climbed out of the pool on shaky legs.

I was exhausted and in desperate need of food, but for the first time in a long time, I felt a sense of accomplishment. It meant a lot to me that a skilled swimmer like Cyrus thought I'd done a good job.

"Thank you," I mumbled as water dripped down my body.

After I pulled off my goggles and swim cap, Cyrus tossed me a towel.

As I ran the towel down my chest and over my stomach, I caught Cyrus watching me out of the corner of my eye.

Poor guy was probably jealous.

In all honesty, though, he had a great body. Broad, strong shoulders, muscular pecs, and a waist that tapered into a V shape before fanning out into his tentacles.

It was probably from all the swimming.

This shit was a workout, that was for sure.

He was still staring as I wrapped the towel around my waist. Being the center of his attention, those wide eyes fixed on me, made me feel unnerved—flustered, even.

"I'll, uh, I'll get changed and we can go. I'll drive if that's okay?"

"Yeah, that sounds good." He put his arms behind his back and shifted on his tentacles.

Gods, this was going to be interesting.

I changed as fast as I could. I'd decided to make myself presentable since we were going out, opting for a short sleeve Henley, khaki shorts, and boat shoes as opposed to my usual athleisure attire.

It was funny I even cared, though, considering Cyrus was essentially always in the nude.

What a weird concept.

I wondered what was underneath that parachute of tentacles.

How did he go to the bathroom?

Did he have a cock?

What the actual fuck?

Was I really thinking about Cyrus's cock?

I shook my head and walked out to the pool deck, where Cyrus was waiting for me by the door.

When he heard my boat shoes clopping against the concrete, he looked in my direction and flashed me those piranha teeth. "Are you sure you don't mind driving?" he asked, looking me up and down.

Fuck.

He was totally checking me out.

I didn't blame him. I looked fucking good. But still, we had an agreement as coach and trainer. I didn't need shit getting weird.

"I don't mind at all. You can be the navigator because I have no clue how to get there."

We walked side by side down the hallway. Well, I walked, and Cyrus did whatever that weird scuffling thing he did was, alongside me.

"How was training?" Atlas asked from behind the desk when we reached the lobby.

I puffed out a harsh breath. "You didn't tell me this guy is an absolute hardass. I haven't had a workout like that in years. That whistle is gonna haunt me in my dreams."

Atlas barked out a laugh. "I told Cyrus you were going to *love* the whistle."

"I think it helped Reece take me seriously. He's already improving. By the time the triathlon rolls around, he'll be the best swimmer in Briar Glenn."

"That title belongs to you, but I'll gladly take second-best swimmer. Hell, I'll take completing the swim with a decent time and moving on to the rest of the race." I smiled, and as if on instinct, I grabbed Cyrus's shoulder and gave it a playful shove.

His skin was so soft and cool underneath my palm, but he wasn't slimy like a fish. It was actually kind of nice. I felt like even more of a dickhead for how I acted at the party, because here I was, giving Cyrus my own innocent little touch.

Atlas looked at where my hand gripped Cyrus and raised his eyebrows, his muzzle curling up in a sly grin.

Gods dammit.

I pulled my hand away and cleared my throat. "Well, we'd better get going."

The wolven smiled even wider. "Oh yeah? Where are you going?"

"We're going to that sushi place over in Acton. You know, the one Fallon loves," Cyrus chimed in.

Did he understand what Atlas was implying?

Or did he just not care?

He was checking me out earlier by the pool...

"I'll let you two get going then. Have a nice lunch."

We said our goodbyes, and the moment we were in the parking lot Cyrus broke the silence. "Was it just me or was he acting weird?"

I stopped dead in my tracks and whipped around to face him. His deep teal coloring was even more impressive in the sun, and I could see myself reflected in the depths of his wide, dark eyes. "Are you fucking oblivious, Cyrus? Atlas thinks this is a date or something."

"Well, is it?" Cyrus asked with a straight face.

"Fuck no!" I blurted out, and the kraken laughed.

"Then why does it matter what Atlas or anyone else thinks?"

"It *doesn't* matter. But, I want to make it clear that we're just two bros going out to get sushi."

Those sharp piranha teeth were on full display with his smile. "Two bros, you say? I didn't realize I was going to lunch with Fallon."

"Oh, fuck off. Don't even compare me to that giant chicken." I rolled my eyes. "Get in the car."

Cyrus's fins flapped slightly as he stifled a laugh. He climbed into the passenger seat beside me, tucking his tentacles into the footwell before clicking on his seatbelt. I was curious how this was going to work, but Cyrus seemed to manage just fine.

"You're insufferable, you know that? Giving me shit in the pool and out of it. A guy can't even catch a break when he's trying to do something nice for you."

"Yes, poor Reece. Getting picked on by a monster. That must be very difficult for you."

"I really am trying, you know." My voice was a shy whisper.

"Hey," he said with a kind smile. "I know you're trying. I wouldn't be here if you weren't."

"WOULD you like to sit at the rotating bar or at a booth?" the hostess asked.

I turned and looked at Cyrus for an answer. I wasn't sure how tentacles would work on a barstool, but I figured it was best not to be presumptuous.

"We'll take a booth, please," he said.

There was so much about Cyrus, and about monsters in general, that was a mystery to me. And for the first time in my life, I wanted to learn more about them.

We shuffled into the booth with me on one side and Cyrus on the other.

"Someone will be over to take your drink order shortly. Enjoy your meal." The hostess set our menus down and returned to the podium at the front of the restaurant.

Cyrus held his menu in his webbed hands, with one tentacle wrapped around each of his arms. The ones he kept wound around his forearms were slightly smaller than the tentacles he used to move, but they were still about the size of my wrist before tapering to a rounded tip. With them coiled, I could see the soft white underside and the quarter-sized suckers covering them.

When he'd grabbed my arm at the party, I'd felt a slight suction from the suckers, almost to the point where there was resistance when I tried to pull away.

Gods, he was interesting.

"I don't even know what to pick. I haven't been here in ages and everything sounds so good." His eyes were unblinking as they scanned the menu.

I bit my lip and stared at my menu, needing to fixate on something other than Cyrus. Something other than the fact that I was out at a restaurant—with a monster.

"Are you a sushi guy or a sashimi guy? I like both, but I tend to prefer sushi. If someone says they don't like the California roll, they're a liar."

Cyrus snorted. "I didn't expect you to be so passionate about sushi."

"What can I say? I enjoy good food. Sweets are my kryptonite, though."

Just as Cyrus was about to say something, the waitress walked up to our table.

"What can I get you to drink?" she asked as she pulled her notepad out of her pocket.

"I'll have a water," I said.

She smiled at Cyrus. "And for you, sir?"

"Could I have a water and a pot of green tea for the table, please?"

"Of course. I'll be right back with those."

"Thank you," Cyrus and I said in unison as the waitress turned on her heel and walked away.

We sat there for a moment, staring at one another.

"So, you're a painter?" I asked. "We didn't really get to talk much about that at the party. Ya know, because I was a jackass."

Cyrus crossed his arms and leaned over the table. "You keep dwelling on that bit. I told you it's fine."

I huffed and shook my head. "It isn't, though. I saw the look on your face, Cyrus. My reaction hurt you." I crossed my arms and leaned back against the vinyl of the booth, my eyes fixed on a family of harpies at the rotating bar.

For some reason, I couldn't bring myself to look at Cyrus. Maybe it was embarrassment over my behavior at the party. Maybe it was because I hated how easily he forgave me, and how willing he was to help me.

"It *did* hurt me," Cyrus said calmly, his voice low and soothing. "But you were a strong enough person to admit you were wrong. You're a strong enough person to want to grow and be better. And look at you, you're accepting help from a monster. You're out to lunch with a monster. You're making leaps and bounds already."

I huffed and rolled my eyes. He acted like that was some impressive feat rather than me using him for my own benefit and then trying to make up for it. I was a piece of work who didn't deserve his kindness. "You're so fucking positive, you know that?"

He shrugged and gave me a small smile. "You aren't the first human to be freaked out by me, and you certainly won't be the last. When you've been around for centuries, you tend to let go of the small stuff."

"Gods. Centuries. I can't even imagine. I'm thirty-five and I already feel like I'm falling apart."

"Thirty-five? Really? You look like you're still in your twenties." He raised his bumpy eyebrows, his coy smile spreading into a wide grin.

I could feel my cheeks turning red.

What the fuck was happening here?

One little compliment from Cyrus and I was blushing like a fucking schoolgirl.

"Oh, fuck off," I grumbled under my breath.

By some act of the goddess, it was at that moment the waitress arrived with our drinks.

"Here you go," she said, putting our glasses in front of us.

She set the fancy cast iron tea kettle on a trivet in the center of the table and placed two dainty cups next to it.

The waitress took our order and quickly bustled off to the kitchen, leaving Cyrus and me alone once again.

I watched in awe as his tentacle unraveled from around his arm and curled around the handle of the teapot, pouring the hot tea into the cup while his hand held it steady.

"Tea?" Cyrus asked as the tentacle reached across the table, the teapot hovering over my cup.

"Please." I stared with wide eyes as the tentacle poured my tea. "That's wild. The painting makes sense now."

Cyrus set the kettle down and laughed. "It's especially convenient for painting. I can use my hands and my tentacles."

"Have you always been an artist? I'd imagine doing the same thing for centuries gets old pretty quick."

Cyrus's tentacle wrapped around his cup and brought it up to his thin lips. "Most of my passions have been art-focused. Sculpting, architecture, photography, but painting is my favorite. There's something satisfying about the act of applying paint to canvas and creating something out of nothing. Taking an image out of my brain and immortalizing it."

I didn't know what to say.

That was some eloquent, poetic shit.

"What about you? How did you come to work for the parks department?"

"I mean, I didn't have too many options. My dad worked for the parks department before me. The old man was actually my boss for a few years. He pretty much decided this was what I was going to do."

Cyrus cocked his head to the side, the bumpy blue skin of his brows wrinkling slightly. "But is that what you wanted?"

If I was being honest, I'd never really thought about it. I'd spent most of my life, at least until my father's passing, doing what he expected of me.

Excelling in sports, graduating at the top of my class, and taking over my father's position at the parks department.

When I tried to think about it now, I had no idea what *I* wanted.

I sat there for a second, staring down at the steam wafting off of my cup of tea and rubbing the back of my neck. "I, uh. I don't really know. I mean, don't get me wrong, I enjoy my job. For the most part, it's pretty easy. But I've always felt like—like there's this void inside of me. Like something's missing, if that makes sense?"

Cyrus took another sip of his tea and nodded. "It makes total sense. I hope you can find what you need to fill that void."

"If I haven't after thirty-five years, I don't think I ever will."

"Oh, you'd be surprised."

Before I could ask Cyrus to explain what he meant, the waitress appeared with our sushi rolls.

"Sorry about the wait!" she said, setting the plates of sushi down on the table.

"That's quite alright. We're not in a rush, are we Reece?"

"No, not at all." I shook my head and stared at Cyrus as he beamed up at the waitress.

Gods, he was so fucking kind to everyone he met.

Even to assholes like me that didn't deserve it.

"Can I get you anything else?"

"I think we're good," Cyrus said as he broke apart his chopsticks with his hands and then passed them along to one of his tentacles.

The thick appendage curled around the delicate sticks and held them perfectly, clicking them together before reaching for a piece of sushi.

I watched as his tentacle carefully brought the sushi up to his mouth. Cyrus's lips parted to reveal two tongues that wrapped around the food and pulled it inside.

My mouth must have been gaping open because Cyrus laughed at me around his mouthful of food. "Ah, yeah. The tongues freak people out a bit, but they're actually quite helpful. Especially for certain *things*."

I could feel myself blushing once again.

Was Cyrus really telling me that two tongues were helpful when it came to oral?

I felt like I was in an episode of *The Twilight Zone*.

Never in my life did I think I'd be out to lunch with a tentacle monster, hearing him talk about how good his tongues were for sucking dick.

I pressed my fingers into my temples and rubbed them hard. "Gods, Cyrus. I don't need to hear all this shit."

He held his arms out in exasperation while his tentacle used the chopsticks to pick up another piece of sushi. "Well, Fallon and I discuss these sorts of things. I was just trying to be friendly."

"Oh, it's friendly alright," I mumbled and shoved a piece of sushi in my mouth.

This fucking kraken was doing things to me—and I didn't hate it.

ELEVEN

Cyrus

My hearts sang as I walked through the front door of my apartment.

I'd spent an entire afternoon with my mate, made him blush several times, and I was under the impression he didn't find me quite as disgusting as I originally thought.

I'd caught him staring at my tentacles and tongues several times throughout our meal—and the look on his face when I told him about the other uses for my tongues —*priceless*.

Gods, he was adorable, and it was so easy to get him riled up too. Some light flirting and the discussion of my unique anatomy, and Reece flushed bright red.

I knew what I'd be painting tonight.

"Fal?" I called out as I shuffled towards the living area. "You home?"

The apartment was dead silent.

I pulled out my phone and texted Fallon.

Me: Should I expect you for dinner?

Sure, I felt like his father most of the time, but I did really enjoy Fallon's company. He'd made the last few years of my life less lonely. Even if he was an annoying prick that didn't know how to cook or clean up after himself.

Fallon: Going out tonight after work. Have a date. Don't expect me until late. How was lunch *eye emoji* *lips emoji* *eye emoji*

I snorted, grinning at the thought of how lunch had gone. I knew Fallon was asking because he'd anticipated it being a disaster.

It was a shame he was such a gossip. I really wished I had someone I could talk to about all of this, but it wasn't worth the risk. Especially with everything going so well.

Me: It was actually quite nice, thanks. I think Reece and I are becoming friends.

Fallon: No. Way. *shocked emoji* The two of you are becoming besties?!

Me: Don't be jealous. No one will ever replace you, baby *kiss face*

Fallon: *crying laughing*

Me: Be safe. Text me if you need a ride later. I'll be home painting.

Fallon: I certainly will, tentacle daddy. *octopus emoji*

I laughed and shook my head. Fallon was too much. But, I guess it made sense that I was tentacle daddy if Atlas was wolf daddy.

With Fallon gone for the night, I'd have the apartment all to myself. I could do anything I wanted.

Anything.

My tentacles propelled me over the carpet and down the hall to my room as fast as they could.

How long had it been since I jerked off? I'd been in such a deep depression that nothing had really done it for me.

But seeing Reece stare at my tongues and my tentacles, those forest green eyes shining bright with lust as a blush blossomed over his pale cheeks. The way water sluiced down over his abs and collected in his happy trail, not to mention the bulge it led to. My mate was truly the most beautiful man I'd ever seen.

He ignited something within me that had been snuffed out some time ago. It made me feel invigorated—*alive.*

I longed for the day I'd taste him, take his cock in my mouth and tease him with my tongues, use my tentacles to explore that sensitive spot inside of him and bring him the type of pleasure that only I could.

Fuck.

The tissue of my mating tentacle swelled, and I scrambled toward my nightstand. I fumbled through the drawers, searching frantically for my stroker.

My eyes caught on the yellow plastic and I snatched it up as fast as I could.

The mating tentacle I kept wrapped around my forearm unraveled, leaving behind a light sheen of lubricant.

I held the stroker in the palm of my hand as my tentacle circled the entrance, coating it with lube before plunging inside.

"Fuck," I groaned, sitting on the edge of my bed.

The silicone was soft and tight, gripping the firm length of my tentacle with each of its thrusts.

I focused my thoughts on Reece, what it would be like to slide my mating tentacle over the defined globes of his ass before slipping it inside of him. The delicious stretch of his tight hole around the tapered length of my tentacle as I eased it inside.

Gods, I hoped he was vers.

He exuded machismo vibes, but from my experience, those were some of the most enthusiastic bottoms.

My tentacle bored in and out of the stroker, the suckers lightly popping and reattaching with each twist and twirl.

It wasn't enough to hurt, but it *was* enough to ramp up the pleasure. I was told it felt amazing on the prostate.

Fuck, how I yearned to play with Reece's prostate, to make him come so hard he'd see stars.

The possibilities were endless.

I could fuck his mouth with one mating tentacle, fuck his ass with the other, and stroke his cock with my hand until we both came.

I bet he tasted like heaven.

My breaths came out as harsh pants and a warm tingle began at the base of my mating tentacle. It spread along the length until it reached the tip.

With a loud groan, I came, my tentacle spasming as it flooded the stroker with a stream of sticky cum.

"Gods damn," I moaned as I flopped back on the bed, doing the best I could to keep my cum from dripping out of the stroker and onto my stomach.

Apparently, all it took to get me off was the thought of what my mate tasted like.

My phone buzzed on the nightstand.

"God dammit, Fallon," I grumbled as one of my tentacles snatched the phone.

Speak of the devil.

It was Reece.

Reece: I had a really nice time at lunch today. Maybe we can grab a coffee together soon?

Tears welled up in my eyes and my hearts thumped wildly in my chest.

This had to be some sort of dream.

Reece Rollins, *my mate*, wanted to spend more time together.

Cyrus: I'd like that.

I clutched my phone against my chest and cried, letting the tears drip down my face and over my fins.

An orgasm and a text message and I turned into a sobbing mess.

But these were happy tears.

For the first time in a long time, I had hope. I had a sense of purpose.

I had something—*someone*—that made my life worth living.

And that felt pretty damn amazing.

TWELVE

Reece

"Oh, you fucking like that don't you," Cyrus rasped against the shell of my ear, the soft pads of his lips tickling my skin with each of his words. *"I knew you wanted me to fuck you from the moment we met. It's the tentacles. It's always the tentacles."*

One of the thick tendrils snaked up my abdomen, over my chest, and around my neck. It squeezed lightly, just tight enough to make speech difficult.

"Tell me what you want, Reece," he whispered as he kissed along my jawline, right where my beard met the column of my neck. His tentacles wrapped over my chest and waist, and he pulled me tighter against him.

The fearful arousal I felt over being at Cyrus's mercy was heady and my cock was so fucking hard.

I wanted him.

No, I *needed* him.

"Please fuck me," I grated out, the words strangled by the pressure on my neck.

Cyrus let out a dark chuckle and nipped playfully at my earlobe, pulling hard enough for me to hiss, but not nearly hard enough to draw blood. His webbed hands slid down my body until they caught on the straps of the lace thong around my hips.

"*Mmm*," he hummed. "*Did you wear this just for me?*"

I'd always had an interest in lingerie—the feel of the fabrics, the stark contrast of lace against a masculine form—but I'd never been with someone I felt comfortable wearing something like that around.

At least, *not until now*.

I gave a slow nod and Cyrus's tongues darted out, licking the side of my face in one slow stroke.

"*We're going to have a lot of fun playing together*." Cyrus tugged the strap of my thong and I moaned as it snapped against my skin with a sharp sting.

He pulled down the thong, freeing my cock from the confines of the lace, rubbing slow circles over my hip to ease the sting.

"*Look at you*," he said as one of his tentacles traveled around the base of my cock. "*You're so fucking pathetic. So horny for a monster*."

"*Cyrus*," I groaned as he pumped my cock with soft, slick strokes.

It was so smooth, and the suckers added a pleasant dragging sensation each time they attached to my skin.

"*Gods, Reece. Your cock is a fucking work of art, you know that? So perfect*." Cyrus swirled his hips against my ass in unison with the strokes of his tentacle. "*And this body. I'm going to enjoy worshiping it. Making you come again and again*."

I whimpered and leaned against him, pushing my ass out, practically begging him to fuck me.

"*So impatient*," he purred as one of his tentacles slid down my back and teased along my crack.

The slick tip found my hole and swirled gently around the entrance, coating it with lube. A moan slipped past my lips as it breached my tight entrance.

"That's it. That's what you needed, wasn't it?" Cyrus asked as the tip of his tentacle swirled inside of me.

"F-fuck yes," I sputtered, my voice hoarse because the tentacle still gripped my neck. *"Harder. Please."*

Cyrus let out another laugh, his fingers tangling in my hair before he wrenched my head back. *"Oh, you want it harder? Deeper, hmm?"*

"Please, Cyrus." I wasn't above begging, at least not for this—not for him.

The tentacle ventured deeper, stretching me around it as it widened, until what I presumed were suckers rubbed against the rim of my hole.

"Tell me you want them."

"I want them," I panted.

"Want what?"

"Your suckers. I want your suckers inside of me." The tentacle stroking my cock squeezed tighter and I groaned. If —when—Cyrus started playing with my prostate, there was no way I was going to last.

"Good boy," he said, and the tentacle lurched forward, twisting and turning as the suckers breached my entrance again and again.

It was like a series of anal beads that could go on and on forever. I'd never felt anything like it.

"Shit!" I moaned and trembled against Cyrus's body.

"See, there's nothing to be afraid of. You're getting tentacle fucked by a monster and you love it, you needy little mess. But I know what you want. You want to feel my suckers on your prostate, don't you?"

The tentacle inside of me continued to thrust in and out, twirling as it did so.

I wasn't capable of coherent speech, so I simply whined and nodded my head against Cyrus's harsh grip on my hair.

"Alright, I guess I'll let you come," Cyrus huffed.

His grip on my neck tightened as the tentacle inside me found my prostate. It swirled mercilessly over the fleshy bead before one of the suckers attached to it—and attached hard.

"Gods damn," I panted, trembling against Cyrus as the suction teased my prostate.

The tentacle on my cock stroked faster and another coiled around my balls to hold them in a tight grip.

"Come with me, baby," Cyrus said and pressed his soft lips against the patch of skin behind my ear.

A tingling sensation started in my balls and a strangled noise crept out of my throat.

My body jolted as I came and thick spurts of cum shot out of my cock, coating Cyrus's tentacles.

"Yes," he moaned.

The tentacle inside of me spasmed, heat spreading as I was filled with his cum.

Slowly, the tentacle around my neck loosened and gently massaged the area where it had strangled me.

I slumped against Cyrus as the last waves of my orgasm washed over me.

"You did so well," Cyrus whispered against my neck. He crossed his arms over my chest, holding me tight against him. *"And when you're ready, we'll do it again."*

"FUCK!" I bolted upright at the sound of my alarm, my mind feeling fuzzy and disoriented.

A pillow was pressed tight to my crotch, and when I slid it away, there was a sizable wet patch covering the front of my briefs.

"Oh, no. Fuck no. No. No. No." I groaned, recalling the dream I had before my alarm woke me up for training.

I threaded my hands through my hair and fell back against my pillows.

This couldn't be happening.

I'd had a wet dream.

About Cyrus.

I didn't even know where to begin when it came to unpacking this.

I mean, these things happened to guys all the time.

I'd had plenty of wet dreams about my friends when I was in high school and even fantasies about weird shit.

But maybe Dream Cyrus was right.

Maybe it was the tentacles.

It was always the tentacles.

What was it Jimenez said the other day about anime? I grabbed my phone from the nightstand and did a quick search for tentacle porn.

There was image after image of tentacles filling orifices. Mouths, pussies, asses. If there was a hole, someone had thought about a tentacle going inside of it.

I scrolled down until an anime video titled "yaoi tentacle monster" caught my attention.

My finger hovered over the clip before I slammed it down hard on my phone screen. I needed to do this.

I had to know.

In the animation, a slender guy was being restrained and spread open like a starfish by a giant tentacle monster.

A tentacle monster that looked terrifying.

It was nowhere near as attractive as Cyrus.

Tentacles slithered over the guy's body until one filled his mouth, another filled his ass, and one stroked his cock.

As the monster worked him over, the little guy whined and groaned, his body bucking against the restraints. I guess to the right person it was hot, but I didn't find it particularly attractive.

I tossed my phone away and clenched my eyes shut, but my thoughts drifted back to my dream.

Of how assertive Cyrus had been, like he was when he trained me.

How his tentacles would feel wrapped around my throat and stroking my cock.

The soft press of his lips against my skin, and how he would feel inside of me.

My cock hardened and strained against the damp material of my briefs.

Fuck.

This was happening.

It wasn't just the tentacles.

It was Cyrus.

THIRTEEN

Cyrus

"Are you sure everything's alright?" I asked Reece as he ran his hands through his wet hair. He'd been a little off recently, avoiding eye contact with me and seeming slightly disinterested in training.

"Yeah, I'm fine. I'm just tired, that's all. Uh, I know we had coffee plans, but can I get a rain check on that? I want to get a nap in before my shift starts. I'd try while we're on rounds, but Jimenez never shuts his damn mouth."

I'd been riding such a high from lunch with him the other day that this felt like a major blow. We'd taken a huge step forward and now it felt like we were taking two steps back.

Maybe the flirting had been too much for him?

But he was the one who texted me about getting coffee...

My expression must have told him what I was thinking.

"Hey," Reece reached out and grabbed my arm, his thumb brushing lightly over my tentacle. "I promise everything is fine. I didn't sleep well. That's all." He gave me a soft smile before he pulled his hand away.

I expected him to wipe his hand on his shorts, like he'd done at the party after we shook hands, but there was none of that.

My mate had offered me a comforting touch and wasn't repulsed by it after the fact.

I nodded my head in understanding, the tentacle he'd touched clenching and relaxing, almost like it was pleased with his attention. "Yeah, wouldn't want you to be tired for your shift. And if you ever need to cancel, just shoot me a text."

He looked down at his feet and shook his head, his cheeks reddening slightly. "Nah, I wouldn't do that. I have a race to prepare for."

He meant that he wouldn't do that to *me*.

It was all starting to make sense now.

The way that Reece looked at me, the shy smiles and blushing cheeks, asking me out for coffee.

Was it possible Reece was interested in me?

As much as that thrilled me, I couldn't help but wonder how that made him feel.

It was hard to let go of misconceptions, to grow and change as a person. Developing feelings for a monster when you'd previously feared them—that was a lot.

Yes, I wanted to be close to my mate, but if he needed space to process things, I was happy to provide him with that.

I'd waited centuries for him, and I'd give him as long as he needed to work through his feelings.

"You get some rest. And uh, if you're bored on rounds later, I always have my phone. If you want to chat." My tentacles clenched my arms tight with anticipation.

"Yeah, I'll shoot you a text for sure. I'll see you tomorrow."

"See ya then."

He gave me a little wave before hiking his bag over his shoulder and walking out of the pool room—but not before Fallon slipped past him.

"Sup, man?" Fallon nodded his head as he trotted past Reece, his tail flicking behind him as he walked. "Yo, Cy," he said, and whistled at me. "How's it going?"

The griffon's feathers were slightly disheveled and his beady eyes were rimmed red.

"It's going. Long night?" I asked as he came to a stop beside me.

He shook his head and clicked his beak. "It was wild, bro. I hooked up with this super hot chick."

"Oh? Is she cuffing season material?" I raised my eyebrows at him, but I already knew what the womanizer was going to say.

"Nah, man. There's no way. She was way out of my league. It was a one-night stand type of deal."

"Did you get her number?"

He looked away and tapped the concrete with his talon. "I, uh, I sort of left before she woke up."

"Fallon, what the fuck? That's low even for you."

"There's no way a chick like her would be into me long term. It was a one-time for curiosity's sake type of thing."

"You're projecting. What Atlas and Tegan have isn't a curiosity's sake type of thing."

He laughed under his breath. "Yeah, but those two are fated mates. It's different. Hot chicks like to fuck me out of curiosity. They want to see what I have going on down there, not spend the rest of their lives trying to kiss someone with a beak. I get it."

It was rare for Fallon to be so vulnerable. Usually, he

carried himself with unshakeable confidence. He must have it bad for this girl.

"I think you should have been a gentleman and said goodbye. Maybe she would have given you her number."

"Cy, I've been through this time and time again. It's better this way."

"If you say so." I sighed, and we both stared at the calm water of the pool.

"How's it been with Reece? Is Ranger Dick following your advice?"

Normally, I'd find a nickname like that funny. However, hearing Fallon speak about my mate that way enraged me— but I did my best to control my anger. Fallon didn't know he was my mate, and he certainly didn't know the real Reece Rollins. "He isn't a park ranger. He works for the parks department. And he isn't a dick, Fal. The whole asshole facade is a front. He's actually quite sensitive."

"Just be careful about getting close to a guy like that. You know he's trying to prove himself with Tegan. He could be using you to look good."

I was fucking livid now.

My color darkened to a deep blue and my fins flared as I rose up on my tentacles until I towered over Fallon.

"Whatever theories you have about Reece, you're wrong. I appreciate the fact that you care about me, but Reece and I are friends, and I won't tolerate you speaking negatively about him." My voice was a sharp hiss, the words slipping out through bared teeth.

"N-Noted," Fallon stammered, shrinking away from me as far as he possibly could.

I took a deep breath to slow my heart rates and lowered down on my tentacles. It wasn't often I lost my temper, but some primal part of me felt fiercely protective of my mate.

"I'm sorry. I didn't mean to lose my shit. I just think there are a lot of misunderstandings when it comes to Reece. He's created this persona of himself that isn't who he actually is."

"If that's what you think, Cy, I believe you. Maybe we can have a boys' night soon. Me, you, Atlas, Reece, maybe Kael. Oh, and Jimenez! That guy seems cool as fuck."

From what I'd heard from Reece, Jimenez and Fallon would likely become best friends.

"We should. I think it would be good for Atlas and Reece to spend some time together. He might feel more relaxed without his sister around."

"Consider it done. I'll talk with wolf daddy and get it all set up."

I snorted. "That reminds me, we have to have a talk about tentacle daddy."

Fallon checked his phone and whistled. "Well, would you look at the time? I have to get to work!"

I laughed as he walked backwards out the door.

"I'll see you at home, tentacle daddy!" He chirped with laughter as he disappeared into the hallway.

FOURTEEN

Reece

My body buzzed with anxiety as I walked through the front door of Leviathan Fitness. I was on edge about seeing Cyrus, about being around him and acting like I wasn't having all of these absurd dreams about him.

I felt bad for canceling our coffee date the other day, but there was no way I could sit across from him and make small talk.

Oh, hey Cyrus! Nice tentacles you've got there. Wanna shove them up my ass?

There was definitely chemistry between us, or at least I thought there was, but I wasn't sure I was ready to pursue anything with him just yet.

And I wasn't even sure if Cyrus was *actually* into me.

He could just be messing with me.

Gods, if I was rejected by a monster I don't think my ego could handle it.

I stopped in front of the pool room and took a deep breath, willing myself to calm down before I stepped through the doorway.

As usual, Cyrus was already there, his smooth body

gliding gracefully beneath the surface of the water. He didn't seem to notice me, so I slipped into the locker room as fast as I could.

Fuck, he looked good when he swam, the lengths of his tentacles rippling as they propelled him through the water.

"Motherfucker," I grumbled as I struggled to pull my jammers over my now semi-erect cock. The things were already tight as fuck, but when you were packing what I was, it was about a thousand times more difficult.

I could already tell today was going to go poorly.

There was no way I could keep doing this to myself.

Sure, I wanted to place well in the triathlon, but this was about more than that. This entire thing with Cyrus was forcing me to examine things about myself that I wasn't sure I was ready to tackle.

I'd have to tell Cyrus I didn't need his help anymore.

After practice today, I'd come up with some excuse and try to end things as painlessly as I could.

When I returned to the pool deck, Cyrus was lying on his back, floating along the surface in the center of the pool.

"Hey there," he said as I approached the edge. "Feeling well rested today?" With ease, he spun forward so that he was facing me and gave me a bright smile.

"Sort of." I rubbed the back of my neck and shifted my gaze off of Cyrus. "I've been having a hard time sleeping."

"Hmm." Cyrus nodded his head. "Well, I guess we're going to have to train harder." He smirked and jetted over to where I was standing. "I thought today I'd watch you from the bottom of the pool. Really get a sense of how your form has progressed and what we can do to improve it. Sound good?"

"Yeah." I shrugged. "If you think it'll help." At least

with him in the water I wouldn't be subjected to that gods awful whistle.

Cyrus tilted his head up at me, his wide eyes narrowing slightly. "Is something bothering you?"

Gods, he was a perceptive fucker.

"Nope." I jumped into the pool, coating Cyrus with a spray of water.

"You're such a wanker," he said the moment my head broke the surface.

"No point in denying it."

Cyrus dove underwater and I stared as his parachute fanned out beneath me.

"Laps. Up and back. Focus on form."

He spoke to me in my head, his sultry British accent spreading warmth throughout my body.

I could already feel my cock straining against my jammers, but if Cyrus noticed, he didn't comment.

How in the ever-loving fuck was I supposed to focus like this?

FOR TWO HOURS, I was subjected to Cyrus's scrutiny. Over and over, he'd chime into my brain and chastise me on my form, my lack of focus, etc. until I decided I'd had enough.

It was too real for me. Too much of a reminder of the things I'd endured during training sessions with my father.

Without a word, I swam over to the side of the pool and climbed the ladder, heading straight for the locker room without even offering Cyrus a glance.

"What was that, Rollins?" Cyrus asked as he burst

through the door of the locker room. "It's like everything we've been working on went right out the window."

I whipped around to face him and held my arms out. "What was with you, Cyrus? You were riding my fucking ass the entire session."

He shuffled closer, rising up onto the tips of his tentacles so he stood slightly taller than me. The normal light blue-green tone of his skin had been replaced by a deep blue, almost black color.

"I was riding your ass because you were acting like you don't even want this," he hissed through sharp, clenched teeth.

I stepped into his space so we were chest to chest, my breaths coming out as labored pants. "You don't know shit about what I want."

"Then why don't you fucking show me," Cyrus snarled, and one of his tentacles darted out to smack the locker right next to my head.

I glared at him, my heart racing as a confusing mixture of adrenaline and arousal coursed through my body.

Cyrus was scary when he was angry, but he was also sort of hot.

Was I really going to do this?

The answer was a resounding yes.

I lurched forward, wrapping my arms around his neck, and slammed my mouth against his so hard our teeth clacked.

"Fuck," he groaned and parted his lips, letting my tongue slip inside.

I felt the cool metal of the lockers against my back as Cyrus pinned me against them and pushed his hips against mine. His tentacles wrapped around my legs, spreading them apart while his hands explored my body.

"Is this what you wanted?" he asked through frantic kisses, thrusting his hips into my already hard cock. "Is this why you couldn't focus?"

"Yes. Holy gods, yes," I moaned as Cyrus kissed his way down my collarbone.

The party. The tension. The dreams.

So much had led up to this moment between us. A moment that a month ago would have seemed like an impossibility.

But there we were—kissing, touching, dry humping one another like we couldn't get enough.

"Tell me." Cyrus broke our kiss to stare at me. His cheeks were flushed dark blue and his chest heaved against mine with each word he spoke. "Tell me where you want to go with this, Reece."

I'd never felt as vulnerable as I felt at that moment, so *exposed*.

But if I was going to do this with anyone, if I was going to push past my fears—if I was going to *fuck* a monster—it was going to be Cyrus.

"I want you to fuck me." My voice was a breathless whisper.

"Oh, thank fuck." Cyrus kissed me again, those twin tongues massaging mine with gentle strokes. "Where?" he asked and gripped my cock through my jammers.

"Ahhh." I groaned against his lips and he laughed. "The shower stall?"

"Mhm," he mumbled.

Before I knew what was happening, Cyrus was *carrying me*, the muscular lengths of his tentacles supporting our combined weight and shuffling us toward the stall without breaking our kiss.

"Holy fuck." I tightened my grip on his neck.

I knew he was strong, but I didn't think he was *that* strong.

"You like that, Rollins?" he asked as his tentacles slammed the door to the shower stall open and we stumbled inside.

"Yes. So fucking hot."

There was something about his physical superiority that did it for me. With Cyrus, I wasn't concerned with being the best. I could just *be*.

"How are we doing this?" I rasped.

In all honesty, I had no fucking idea about kraken anatomy. I mean, I'd had those dreams, but for all I knew, Cyrus could be packing a monster cock under that parachute.

He broke our kiss and ran his webbed hand along my jaw. "Well, I didn't anticipate having this conversation today, but I don't really have any holes that are fuckable. So, if you want to top, you can fuck my mouth."

Shit.

I bet those tongues would feel amazing milking every last drop of cum out of my cock, but that wasn't what I wanted right now.

I wanted Cyrus to fuck my brains out.

"No," I huffed, getting impatient. "I told you I wanted you to fuck me." I rotated my hips against his. "Do you have a cock under there—or?"

Cyrus laughed again and unraveled the tentacles he kept wrapped around his arms. "I don't have a cock, but I have these." The tentacles wriggled in the air playfully. "My hectocotylus, my mating tentacles."

Oh my gods.

Those were his *cocks*.

"So you're fucking telling me, the first time we met, you

touched me with your cock." Realization hit. "You fucking touch everything with your cock!"

"Will you relax? It isn't the same for my kind. Now, do you want me to fuck you or not?" He raised one of his bumpy eyebrows in question.

Yeah, it was weird—*different*—but even with that little detail about his tentacles, my cock was still throbbing. I still wanted him more than I'd ever wanted anything in my entire life.

"Where do you want me?"

Cyrus smiled, pressing his lips to mine one last time before his tentacles spun me around to face the shower wall.

My fingers scrambled to pull down my jammers, but the wet material clung to my skin.

"Let me help you," Cyrus purred in my ear. He slid his hands down my chest and over my stomach before slipping them beneath the band of my jammers.

"Motherfucker," I groaned as he worked them off my waist.

My cock jutted forward, smearing precum on the shower wall as his tentacles pulled the swimsuit down over my muscular thighs.

Cyrus pressed against my back and gripped my cock, using the palm of his hand to spread my precum down my shaft before giving it a few slow pumps.

"Your cock is just as pretty as you are, Reece. I can't wait to suck you off and watch that handsome face as you come undone. Would you like that?"

He pumped faster and a tentacle slid over my chest before settling on top of my nipple. The suckers coating the underside latched on and I let out a low moan, throwing my head against Cyrus's shoulder and thrusting into his hand.

"You would like that. Look at you. A monster fucker

too. It must be genetic." He laughed against my neck before dragging the pointed tips of his teeth over my skin.

"Cyrus, please."

I'd dreamt about this. I'd beg and plead for it if I had to.

"Alright, alright, Rollins. It's coming." The firm length of his mating tentacle slid down my crack and I clenched my ass tight, stopping it from reaching my hole.

"Relax for me," he whispered, rubbing his free hand along my jaw. "It's self-lubricating. It'll go in nice and easy."

Self-lubricating.

I took a deep breath, focusing on the feel of Cyrus's hand on my cock as the tip of his tentacle circled my hole, coating it in a layer of lube.

His mating tentacle slowly pushed inside and my breath hitched.

Fuck.

It was so smooth. The familiar stretch was there, but there was none of the resistance that came with a human cock, at least not yet.

"Breathe, darling. You're doing so well."

Darling.

I'd never been called something so sweet.

Cyrus nuzzled against my shoulder as the tentacle worked its way in deeper. There was none of the feral thrusting I was used to. Cyrus's body remained still as he calmly assaulted my ass. "You're almost to the suckers. Do you want them?"

My thoughts went straight to my dream and what those fleshy anal beads had felt like slipping in and out of me again and again.

It was enough to have my balls tightening up and a tingling sensation forming at the base of my spine.

"Please," I whimpered through clenched teeth. "I don't know how long I'm going to last though."

Living out this sexual fantasy was proving to be a lot for me.

"Shh," Cyrus whispered. "That doesn't matter. I want you to enjoy this. I want it to be good for you."

And it was. More than good, actually.

When was the last time I'd been with someone who actively wanted sex to be enjoyable for me? It was usually just random hookups where both parties selfishly chased their own release as fast as possible.

This was different, though, just like everything with Cyrus was.

He put my comfort and my pleasure before his own.

Cyrus pushed in further, my tight entrance throbbing as the soft suckers ventured deeper.

"Cyrus," I moaned, arching my back and thrusting my cock into his fist.

"That's it, my needy boy. I'll give you what you want."

He continued jerking my cock with rough tugs, and the moment the tip of his mating tentacle pulsed over my prostate, I came with a loud groan, coating his hand and the shower wall with streams of cum.

"There it is," Cyrus said as he kissed along my neck, stroking me through my orgasm until I went limp against his chest.

FIFTEEN

Cyrus

I gently slid out of Reece before finishing with a low moan, my mating tentacle spasming and painting the dimples on his lower back with thick streaks of cum.

Considering he had work after this, I thought coming *on* him instead of *in* him was the polite thing to do. Although, the thought of my cum leaking out of him all day, marking him as mine, appealed to me on a primal level.

"Can I clean you up?" I asked, reaching in front of Reece to start the shower.

"Sure," he mumbled.

The waterfall showerhead coated us in a light spray of warm water, rinsing away our cum and the lube left behind from my mating tentacle. I pumped body wash out of the wall mount dispenser and into my hand, creating a sudsy lather before I rubbed it over the corded muscles of Reece's body.

"Gods damn," he groaned, leaning into my touch. "That feels nice."

"I'm glad you think so. Aftercare is important."

Reece let out a shy laugh. "I, uh, don't have much experience with that."

Well, I had a lot to make up for then.

When we were all clean, I shut off the tap and turned us around until my back was braced against the shower wall and Reece rested on my chest.

I couldn't believe this was happening.

My mate had initiated this between us.

He'd wanted this.

Wanted me.

"Is this okay?" I asked, knowing how he felt about touching.

"S'good," he mumbled and brought his muscular arm up to wrap around the back of my neck. His fingers softly brushed my fins and I shuddered.

Lying collapsed on top of one another in a shower stall wasn't exactly romantic, but it was the best aftercare I was able to offer at present.

"Sorry if I went a little overboard today with training."

Reece shook his head against my chest. "You didn't go overboard. It just—reminded me of something. Well, someone."

"Of who?"

His deep laugh echoed off the tile walls. "Gods, Cyrus. You really want to make me come harder than I have in my entire life, then grill me about my childhood trauma?" His fingers traced back and forth over the fins along my neck. "Can we at least go out to dinner first? Or maybe fuck in a bed?"

"I want to make sure I do better next time, is all. We don't have to talk about it right now." I ran my hand along his stomach and through his happy trail. "And I'd very much like to take you out to dinner and then fuck you in an actual bed."

"Awfully presumptuous of you to assume that this is going to happen again."

"Well, is it going to happen again?"

Reece turned so he was facing me, propping himself up with his elbow on my chest.

"I mean, I'd like it to." He paused for a second, digging his teeth into his lower lip before he glanced up at me with those emerald eyes. "I like you, Cy. And no matter what I keep telling myself or how hard I try to deny it, the thoughts I have about you, the feelings, they won't go away. Something about you, *about this*, is different."

"Did you ever think it might be you that's different too? You've grown so much, Reece."

He looked down and smiled. "You think so?"

"I mean, the Reece Rollins I first met would have never fucked a monster."

His cheeks turned crimson and he rubbed his fingers along his temple. "Shut up."

"Come here, my little monster fucker." I used my tentacle to bring his head forward until his mouth connected with mine.

"Fuck you," Reece grumbled against my lips.

"I'd happily go again." And I could, as many times as my mate wanted.

"I need to get going soon or I'm gonna be late for work," he said, slowly pulling away.

"Right, right. Parks department stuff. Got it. Forgot that some people have normal jobs."

Reece stiffly rose to his feet and I shuffled to a standing position next to him.

"Here." I passed him his jammers.

"Thanks."

He cracked open the door of the shower stall and stuck his head out, checking to make sure the locker room was clear.

Satisfied, he slipped out of the stall with his jammers covering his cock, and I followed behind him.

I still couldn't believe this had happened, and even though Reece admitted to wanting to do it again, I wasn't exactly sure what this meant for the two of us. Obviously, I knew this didn't make us a couple, but how were things going to go moving forward?

I was admiring the way Reece's ass flexed as he pulled on his briefs when he turned around to face me.

"Listen..." He scrubbed his hand along the back of his neck.

I clenched my jaw, bracing for impact.

There was no way something good was going to come out of this. If he wasn't ready, he wasn't ready...

"I want to keep training with you, and—" He motioned between the two of us. "I want to keep doing this." His voice was a shy whisper, his cheeks flushed bright red. "But I'd like it if we could keep this between the two of us."

I blinked my eyes rapidly, in total shock at what my mate was saying. I opened my mouth to speak but Reece cut me off.

"I don't mean forever, but for right now. I, uh, this is all so new. I need some time to wrap my head around things."

"I understand completely."

I'd give him an eternity if he needed it. I was just happy he didn't immediately regret this.

Reece pulled his shirt over his head and stepped into my space. "Thank you."

He stared at me for a moment before sliding his hand

along the back of my head and pressing his lips to mine in a quick kiss. "I'll text you later, okay?"

"I'd like that." My tentacle trailed along his arm as he pulled away.

"Bye."

"Bye."

He gathered his things then slipped out the door, leaving me alone in the locker room.

"Fuck," I mumbled under my breath and sat down on the bench between the rows of lockers.

A mixture of emotions swirled around my head.

I'd fucked my mate for the first time in the shower stall of my best friend's gym.

What a whirlwind.

Reece's strange behavior over the past few weeks finally made sense.

He had been avoiding me because he was attracted to me.

It was like a weight lifted off of me, and for the first time in a long time, I felt lighter. I was beginning to think that maybe my hopes and dreams about what Reece and I could be weren't so far-fetched after all.

SIXTEEN

Reece

"What's got you in such a good mood today?" Jimenez asked as I passed him his coffee.

"What do you mean?" I said, taking a sip of my coffee and forcing myself not to smile.

Yeah, I'd had a pretty fucking great morning, but I wasn't about to kiss and tell.

At least not yet.

And definitely not to Jimenez.

"I don't know. You were, like, whistling and shit when I picked you up. It's very out of character for you."

"What are you, a detective or some shit, Jimenez? I had a good training session this morning, that's all."

Fought with my trainer. Kissed him. Got tentacle fucked. You know, a typical Wednesday. Nothing too crazy.

"Alright, alright. Where am I going?" he asked as he pulled the work truck onto the main road that ran through Briar Glenn.

"The parks have been pretty clean. Why don't we head back to the office for a little bit? I need to catch up on some paperwork."

To be honest, we spent the majority of our time on the job cruising around, checking on the parks and playing fields.

It wasn't the most exciting job, but someone had to do it.

"Sounds good, boss man. I wanna browse my dating apps anyway."

"Jimenez, what the fuck are you doing on dating apps?"

"It's rough out here, man. You'd know that if you weren't committed to a life of celibacy." Jimenez glanced over at me. "You should let me make you a profile. It's like the wild west of dating. You can keep swiping and swiping. But I swear to the gods if I see one more person holding a dead fish in their profile pic..." He clenched the steering wheel tight and shook his head.

"Nah, I'm good, thanks. I have enough shit going on in my life as it is."

"You really don't, though. You never get lonely?" He pulled the truck to a stop in front of the building we shared with the fire department and the library before looking over at me.

I thought about it for a moment.

Yeah, I missed having sex on the regular, but I was never someone that had to have a partner. I'd never felt a deep enough connection with anyone to want to keep them around for more than just the occasional hookup.

And I'd never been in love, that was for fucking sure.

But presently, there was someone in my life I enjoyed being around. Someone who made me laugh with his stupid fucking flirting and made me come with his stupid fucking tentacles.

"I mean, sometimes I do, but I figure if I meet someone, I meet them. I'm not joining a dating app though. It's just not my thing."

Jimenez shot me that winning smile, all white teeth and perfect fucking dimples. "You're old school. I can appreciate that. A gentleman from a bygone era."

"Oh, fuck off, Jimenez." I stepped out of the truck, leaving him cackling behind me.

BUZZ.

Buzz.

I quickly snatched my phone from where it sat on my desk.

About time.

I'd been waiting for Cyrus to text me all fucking morning.

I guess I could have texted him first, but I didn't want to seem too desperate.

I leaned back in my chair and peeked through the glass panel of my office door. Jimenez was slumped over his desk, mouth gaping open with light snores slipping out. It was probably the only time the guy wasn't attractive.

Confident I wouldn't be bothered, I unlocked my phone and read the message.

Cyrus: Hey there. I thought you were going to text me. I was getting impatient.

I bit my lip and grinned down at my phone screen. Apparently, we were both playing the waiting game. I felt a slight sense of satisfaction that Cyrus was the first one to crack. Call it my competitive spirit or whatever.

Reece: Maybe I wanted you to text me first.

Cyrus: Gods, I get you off AND I have to text first? I can already tell that there's going to be an uneven distribution of work here.

Reece: What can I say? I'm a pillow princess *princess emoji*

There was some truth to that statement.

Don't get me wrong, giving was great, but so was receiving with the absolute least amount of work necessary.

Cyrus: I gathered as much. What are you doing right now?

Reece: Sitting in my office. You?

Cyrus: Thinking about how good your ass felt stretched around my tentacle, if I'm being honest.

"Fuck," I mumbled, and ran my fingers through my hair. One little reminder of what we'd gotten up to this morning was all it took to have my cock standing at attention.

Reece: You felt so fucking good. I'm pretty sure I have marks on my nipple from your tentacle.

Cyrus: Oh yeah? Show me those nips.

I snorted. *Nips.*

Reece: I'm at work.

Cyrus: Show me.

I leaned back in my chair to get another look at Jimenez. He was still fast asleep.

Was I really going to send Cyrus nudes while I was at work?

Yes, yes I absolutely was.

I quickly closed the blinds to my office, clicked the lock, and started to unbutton my shirt.

This was crazy.

But it was also exciting.

I liked it when Cyrus was dominant and demanding. It made me want to please him.

I stood in front of the mirror and opened my shirt. Light purple sucker marks trailed across my chest before turning into a deep purple bruise right over my nipple.

The fucker had given me a purple nurple.

I was going to have to wear a shirt in the pool until these faded. All it would take was one look from someone at the gym to know what the two of us had gotten up to.

My phone buzzed again.

Cyrus: I'm waiting.

I flexed my arm, pushing out my bruised pec, and snapped a picture. Before sending it over, I added the caption 'look what you did to my fucking nipple.' Cyrus replied almost immediately.

Cyrus: That's a good boy. Fuck. I can't wait to suck on those nipples while I jerk your cock.

"Shit," I hissed and palmed my dick through my pants.

I mean, the door was locked and Jimenez was passed the fuck out. And I was the boss. I didn't need to explain myself.

I bolted over to my desk and threw myself down onto the chair. My fingers fumbled with my belt and I cursed under my breath as I fought to pull down my zipper.

"Fuck," I groaned the moment my hand made contact with my already throbbing cock.

A bead of precum formed along the slit of my head as I worked my cock with slow strokes. With my free hand, I typed out a message to Cyrus.

Reece: I'm touching myself under my desk.

Fuck, I loved being a tease.

Cyrus: Show me.

It was too easy. I knew he'd play along.

I set my phone to record and sent Cyrus a video of me smearing my precum over my head with my thumb before giving my cock two quick jerks. You could hear my heavy breaths in the background of the clip.

Cyrus: So obedient. So fucking filthy. Stroke that cock and imagine me bending you over your desk and fucking you.

I loved seeing this side of Cyrus. It was such a stark contrast to his usual playful demeanor.

I leaned back in my chair, digging my teeth into my lower lip, thinking about what it would feel like with those tentacles pinning me to my desk while Cyrus used his suckers to massage my prostate. What it felt like as each row of suckers worked in and out of my ass.

My balls were already tingling with the urge to come.

Reece: I wish you were inside of me right now.

My phone buzzed with a message from Cyrus. It was a link to a blue-green silicone dildo.

A silicone dildo that was shaped like a tentacle.

Cyrus: Send me your address. I want you to use this and think of me.

Fuck. My kraken—*whatever it is he was*—was sending me a tentacle dildo to use and think of him. I was positive there would be stipulations with this gift, in the form of me sending Cyrus videos of me fucking myself with it.

And I was more than okay with that.

"F-Fuck," I stammered and came with a deep groan, catching the thin ribbons of cum with a tissue before they could drip down onto my pants.

My phone vibrated as my body jerked with the last few waves of my orgasm. I wiped my hands, tucked my cock back into my pants, and threw away the cum-soaked wad of tissues before opening my phone.

It was another text from Cyrus.

Cyrus: Did you come?

Holy fuck, did I.

Reece: Yeah

Cyrus: What were you thinking about?

Reece: Using my new toy for you.

Cyrus: Good boy.

SEVENTEEN

Cyrus

For the next two weeks, Reece and I trained, fucked, and joined one another for lunch and coffee dates. During the moments we weren't together, we spent our time texting, and I'd learned a lot about my mate.

His middle name was Michael and he loathed wearing socks; he said he hated the way they felt on his feet. He ran track in high school and he shaved his chest hair each time he took a shower to avoid the annoying prickle of regrowth.

They were tiny, mundane things, but I enjoyed knowing them, knowing *him*.

And I particularly enjoyed the Reece Rollins he kept locked tight under that tough facade.

He was terrified of buzzing insects, swatting and cursing at them as if they threatened his very existence. On walks, he had to stop and pet every dog, and for being a triathlete fitness freak, he had quite the sweet tooth.

After sex, he'd snuggle up against me and run his fingers over the fins on my face while he stared into my eyes.

He was sensitive.

Nuanced.

And with each passing day, I could feel myself falling in love with him.

Sure, part of that inextricable pull to Reece was the mating bond, but it was also due to who he was as a person.

The sun was starting to rise as I pulled my car to stop outside Reece's house. This morning we'd head down to the shore of the lake for his first open-water swim.

I was convinced he was ready. He'd been pushing himself quite hard now that I could use sex as a training incentive, but I'd seen his face when I suggested it.

The cold temperature of the water, the slight waves, maintaining his location. Anyone would find it intimidating, but if he was going to place well in this triathlon, we needed to start practicing under the conditions he was going to experience.

Reece stepped out of the house dressed in his jammers and a hoodie, with the hood covering most of his head except for a tuft of red hair.

Gods, my mate was a stud.

I muttered a thank you to the goddess as he slipped inside my car.

"Morning," I said.

"Morning," he grumbled back.

It appeared my mate wasn't much of a morning person. I knew he had an unhealthy caffeine addiction, and I'd promised to take him for coffee as soon as we were done with our session.

Reece scanned the empty street for a moment before he leaned over and wrapped his hand behind my head, pulling me in for a kiss.

He slipped his tongue inside of my mouth and I groaned against his lips as I rubbed my tongues along his.

"Well, that was certainly a development," I said with a sigh as he pulled away and fastened his seatbelt.

"What? I missed you," he mumbled under his breath, pushing back his hood. "I can be sweet sometimes."

He squinted at me in the dim lighting before wetting his thumb with his tongue and running it over my eyebrow. "Were you painting?" he asked and showed me the streak of gold on his thumb.

I wanted to say yes, to tell him I'd been working on a portrait of him in his parks department uniform, but he'd find out soon enough.

That is, if I ever worked up the courage to invite him to my gallery show.

Sometimes it was best to keep the muse and the art separate.

"Yeah, I'm working on a few different pieces. I've been quite inspired lately."

Inspired by the beauty of my mate.

By you.

"I'd like to see your work sometime. You know, if you're comfortable sharing it with me or whatever. I know how people can be about their art."

A smile spread over my face and my hearts sang over the fact that Reece was interested in seeing what I created. For now, I'd hold off on the paintings of him, but I'd be happy to show him some of my older work. There was certainly enough of it.

I put the car in drive and started down the road toward the lake.

"How are you feeling this morning?"

"Tired. Not ready to jump in that cold ass water." He nestled deeper into his hoodie and I laughed.

"It's only going to get worse as we get closer to the triathlon. Best to get used to it now."

"Yeah, you're right." His hand snaked over the center console and came to rest on one of my tentacles, his thumb rubbing tiny circles over my smooth skin.

Without saying a word, I gripped the steering wheel with my left hand and grabbed Reece's hand with the other.

THE LIGHT of the morning sun shone bright red on the lake's surface as the waves lapped against the shore. Other than the two of us, the park was empty.

Reece stretched for a few moments before pulling his hoodie over his head, putting that perfect body on display.

"Gods damn!" he bellowed and threw his hoodie down by my feet. "How can you not wear clothes?" He rubbed his palms over his biceps with rough strokes.

"My body thermoregulates. Nifty little monster trick. Unfortunately, the trade-off is looking like this." I fanned my tentacles around me playfully and Reece stepped closer.

He wrapped his arms around my neck and pulled me close, the pointed tips of his nipples rubbing against my chest.

"I happen to think you're quite attractive," he said and pressed his forehead to mine.

I had trouble believing a gorgeous man like him found a creature like me attractive.

"Reece Michael Rollins has the hots for a monster. I better alert the masses."

He blushed slightly and his tongue darted out to wet his lips. "Soon, Cy. It isn't gonna be like this forever."

To be honest, I didn't mind if it was. As long as we

could keep going with whatever this was between us, with whatever made my mate comfortable, I was happy.

"I'll be here. Take all the time you need, darling."

He brushed his lips against mine, his hands traveling down to where my back met my tentacles, and lightly thrust his cock into my hips.

"You're stalling," I mumbled against his mouth with a laugh. "What if someone sees us?"

"They won't. But yeah, I am stalling."

"If you're a good boy and do your swim, I promise I'll get you a coffee and get you off."

"Fuck," he groaned into my mouth before pulling away.

He could be such a brat. But he was *my* brat.

"Do you want me to get in with you?" I asked as Reece pulled on his swim cap and goggles.

"Nah, I won't subject you to that. Just have a towel ready for me when I'm done."

He stepped closer to the water, hissing the moment it hit his toes.

"You need to just get it over with. Jump right in." It was easy enough for me to say that from the comfort of the shore.

Reece clapped his hands together twice, and with a hoarse yell, he jumped into the lake.

"Motherfucker!" he howled the moment his head popped up from below the surface. "S'fucking cold."

"The sooner you start swimming the sooner it'll be done, Rollins," I yelled, my voice echoing out over the lake.

Reece got into position, and I started the timer on my phone as he swam out to the buoy.

He'd made leaps and bounds in his training. It was evident in how his arms moved, and how his body cut through the water.

With steady strokes, he pushed himself, but as he reached the center of the lake, he suddenly cried out and his head bobbed underneath the water.

I watched for a moment until he resurfaced, his arms flailing wildly as he yelled out to me.

Panic set over me as I tossed my phone, rushing to the edge of the lake.

I'm coming. Hold on. I'm coming.

I spoke to him in his head, trying my best to calm him, to keep my voice steady and even.

But I was absolutely terrified.

I plunged into the cool water, the muscles in my tentacles rippling as I shot off toward Reece.

A swim that took him a considerable amount of time was nothing for me, and I was able to find him easily with his thrashing and sputtering.

I breached the surface and wrapped him up in my tentacles, pulling his back tight against my chest. "I'm here, darling. I've got you. I've got you," I said as he coughed.

"Cramps. I c-couldn't kick."

His legs had cramped, and in his panic, he'd sucked in a decent amount of water.

My mate had been in danger, and I'd just been standing on the beach watching.

"Shh. I've got you," I whispered in his ear as I swam us back to shore.

The moment I could stand, I rose on my tentacles and dragged Reece up onto the shore.

"Fuck," I shouted once I got a better look at him.

He was shivering and coughing like mad.

I scuttled to the parking area and started my car, cranking the heater and grabbing extra towels.

"Shit. Shit. Shit," I mumbled, pulling Reece into my arms and covering him with towels.

At the moment, I didn't give a fuck if anyone was around to see us.

"I am so, so sorry," I mumbled with my lips pressed against his temple. "I should have swam out with you." My voice was strangled. I was on the verge of tears.

"S'okay, Cy. Not your fault." He snuggled closer against my chest and my tentacles tightened their grip on his body.

He didn't understand, though.

He was my mate, and I wouldn't be able to live with myself if something happened to him.

We sat like that for a few minutes, two males huddled together on a cool beach as the morning sun crested overtop of us.

Under other circumstances, it would have been beautiful, romantic even, but I felt like shit.

"Thank you for swimming out to get me." Reece strained against my tentacles and stretched out his legs. "I think I can make it to the car now."

I nodded, handed Reece his hoodie, and we wordlessly trudged across the beach to my car.

"I think I'm going to withdraw," Reece said the moment I slammed the car door shut.

His hood was pulled over his head and he stared at the lake with a blank expression plastered on his face.

"Reece." I slid my hand over his thigh and he looked at me with bloodshot eyes. "Today was a one-off thing. I know it was scary, but I don't think you should withdraw from the race."

"That was shit, Cy. What's the point of entering if I'm going to have a shit time?"

He'd worked so hard preparing for this.

We'd worked so hard preparing for this.

And he was going to quit?

"This isn't about cramping or almost drowning, is it?"

He didn't answer me, he simply turned and looked out the window.

"If you don't talk to me, Reece, I can't help you. And I *want* to help you. So please, please, talk to me. Don't give me that hardass bullshit that you feed everyone else because I know better."

He turned to face me, his cheeks flushed red and tears already forming in the corners of his eyes. "Do you know why I got out of the pool that day?"

I'd had a lingering suspicion for some time now, but I shook my head no. I wanted—no, *needed*—to hear it from him.

"The way you were training me, yelling at me, it reminded me of him. Reminded me of my father." He rubbed his eyes, smearing the tears over those perfect light-red eyelashes. "My entire life, he raised me to be the best. It was a given. Expected of me. And if I wasn't, the old man rode my ass about it. But for Tegan, it was different. He was always telling her how proud he was. How amazing she was."

Tears streamed down his cheeks and he sniffled.

"I did everything he wanted, to the best of my abilities, and it was never enough. A lot of my issues are because of him. When I was a kid, back before the integration, I had a run-in with a monster that scared the fuck out of me. And my father? He didn't fucking believe me. *He made fun of me.* That really fucked me up, Cy. You know, there was a part of me that was happy when he passed. I feel like shit actually saying it out loud, but it's true. It was like this weight had been lifted. I could let go of all his expectations.

But then, when the integration happened, I was forced to face one of my biggest fears and all these feelings about monsters and my father got dredged up again. I was that same scared little boy."

Reece had been through so much. That incident with the monster and his father's continuous verbal abuse had done serious damage. He'd developed that prickly demeanor as a defense mechanism. He'd coped the best way he knew how...

"And with you, Cy, at first I didn't even give you a fucking chance. I was such a dickhead to you. I didn't deserve your help or your kindness, but you gave it to me anyway. I started to have this attraction to you, and yeah, at first that scared me too. I told myself we were just fuck buddies or whatever, but it's grown into so much more than that."

He looked at me, his face bright red, those green eyes looking the prettiest I had ever seen them.

"I enjoy every second we spend together, whether you're fucking me or blowing that fucking whistle at me. I'm not scared anymore. I don't give a fuck that you're a monster. I have feelings for you, Cyrus, and I'm sorry it took a near-death experience for me to admit that."

I lurched over the center console and wrapped my arms around him tightly.

Seeing him like this broke me. My mate had been carrying all of this for so long.

"You're going to do great, you know that right?"

"But what if I don't?" he asked, his head buried in the crook of my neck.

"As long as you give it your all, that's what matters. That's something to be proud of."

EIGHTEEN

Reece

"Shit," I mumbled under my breath, holding one shirt against my chest and then the other.

Someone once told me the Henley shirt was the top equivalent of gray sweatpants, and I'd held onto that, loving the way the thin material stretched tight over my broad chest.

I knew Cyrus was a fan of that too.

Since my near-death experience and slight emotional breakdown, things had been going great between us. I could be vulnerable around Cyrus in a way that I couldn't with other people. I didn't have to hide my thoughts or feelings.

He felt *safe*.

There was no way we could do this forever—and I'd never ask him to. We'd have to go public with our relationship soon. But for now, I was content to keep what we had between the two of us.

I wanted to savor this period where we wouldn't have to answer any questions or deal with judgment.

I'd changed, and Cyrus was the driving force behind that.

Grabbing my phone, I sent him a text.

Reece: I need your help. I don't know what to wear.

Cyrus: Send me pics.

I held up one shirt, snapped a pic, then repeated it with the other before sending them over to Cyrus.

Cyrus: Yeah, but send me one without the shirt in the way. Shirts are optional for boys' night. *one-hundred emoji*

I snorted and rolled my eyes. Gods, he was such a horny fuck.

Tonight would be my first time over at the apartment Cyrus shared with Fallon, and our first time around a large group of people since we started getting intimate.

I was nervous, but also excited. I loved teasing Cyrus, and this would be the perfect opportunity to head over there looking like a snack.

When I was finally dressed, my beard freshly trimmed and my hair pushed back in that messy way Cyrus liked, I grabbed my keys and typed out a quick text.

Reece: Leaving now. See you soon.

I stared at my phone for a second. Would adding a kiss emoji be too much? I mean, we kissed in person. We did more than kissing in person.

Fuck it.

Reece: Leaving now. See you soon. *kissy face emoji*

Cyrus: See you soon, darling. *kissy face emoji*

Darling.

I could feel my cheeks heating, like they did every time he called me that. I wasn't used to pet names or being with someone that made me *feel* things.

It was at that moment I realized this was something different. That what Cyrus and I had was real.

And I was thrilled about it.

"YOOO. LOOK WHO'S HERE." Fallon whistled, and clapped me on the back as I stepped into the apartment.

Gods, he was such a fucking frat boy.

I could tolerate him for Atlas and Cyrus, but I'd never go out of my way to hang out with him one-on-one.

Jimenez was enough for me.

Speaking of Jimenez...

"Yooo!" he shouted from inside the apartment, raising his beer at me when I came into view.

"Hey." I gave him a slight tilt of my chin.

I scanned the apartment, taking in its high ceilings and exposed brick walls. When I pulled up to the building, I knew it was going to be fancy, but this was nicer than I'd expected.

Cyrus must do well because there was no way Fallon could afford this on what he made at the gym.

My—*whatever Cyrus was to me*—the artist.

Speaking of art, the walls of the apartment were covered with paintings.

I stepped closer to a piece that depicted a sunrise over the water. It reminded me of the morning Cyrus and I had spent together down by the lake several weeks before.

The morning where I'd almost drowned and then confessed my feelings for Cyrus.

"Cy painted that one a few weeks ago. It's good, isn't it?" Fallon asked and ruffled his feathers.

I nodded, smiling to myself.

Cyrus was a shithead. Keeping these from me.

I wondered what other secrets he had.

"You want a drink, Reece?" Fallon asked, his head buried inside the fridge. "Tegan mentioned you don't like booze, so I had Cyrus pick up some seltzers and he made this fancy mocktail thing."

I fucking lived for mocktails.

And Cyrus knew that.

"I'll try the mocktail, thanks." I glanced at the living area before I took a seat at the kitchen island. "Where are Atlas and Cyrus?"

Jimenez joined me and leaned against the island.

"They're out on the balcony. You gotta ask for a tour, man. This place is fucking nice."

"That's all Cyrus. This place is way outta my price range," Fallon said as he poured my drink. He held the pitcher with the scaly skin of his talons.

Shit.

He was pretty fucking good with those little chicken hands.

Fallon passed me my drink and walked around the island. "I invited our buddy Kael from the gym, but he had plans, so it's just the five of us tonight. Let's head out to the terrace." He said terrace in a gods awful British accent, obviously mocking Cyrus and the way he said it.

I knew he was trying to be funny, but it still made my fist clench.

Jimenez and I followed Fallon across the living room and through wide sliding glass doors that led out to the terrace.

The sun was setting, bathing the terrace that overlooked Briar Glenn in warm, orange light. Atlas leaned against the railing, his muzzle scrunched up as he let out a barking laugh at something Cyrus said.

Cyrus.

Hearing that smooth British accent sent shivers down my spine.

He looked in our direction as we walked out onto the patio, and when his gaze connected with mine, his mouth parted into a wild smile.

He was so fucking handsome.

Not in the traditional sense, sure, but in a way that was attractive to me.

The angular planes of his face, his soft translucent fins,

the musculature of his body, his bright coloring, and *those tentacles.*

Nothing would ever compare to those tentacles.

"Hey there," Atlas said, extending his hand out to me.

I was expecting a handshake, but the wolven pulled me in for a tight hug.

Holy fuck, he was strong.

I was shocked he hadn't accidentally suffocated my sister with one of his hugs.

"Hello, Reece." Cyrus's voice was so calm it practically bordered on a purr. I watched as he brought his mocktail to his lips and winked at me.

That fucker.

And I was so sure that I was the one that was going to be doing the teasing.

The five of us sat on the fancy outdoor sectional, posh as Cyrus called it, drinking and shooting the shit.

I was surprisingly relaxed—until Atlas brought up the triathlon.

"How's tri training coming along, Reece?" Atlas asked, leaning forward in his seat. "I know you and Cyrus have been hitting it pretty hard." He glanced over at Cyrus and I could have sworn he smirked, but it passed too quickly for me to be sure.

Was the wolven onto us? I knew there were cameras in the gym, but the locker room and showers were safe. There was no way Cyrus would have mentioned to him what was going on between us without bringing it up to me first.

"There's what, a month left until the race?" the wolven asked.

Gods, Atlas. Way to remind me.

Cyrus chimed in before I could answer. "Yeah, a month.

Reece is going to do great. He's come a long way. A few more open water swims and he'll be set."

I fought to school my expression. I didn't want to give anything away, but knowing that Cyrus believed in me made my heart sing.

"We'll all be there to cheer you on. I think your mom and your sister are making shirts for everyone." Atlas wiggled his ears.

I choked on my drink. "Are you fucking serious?" I coughed.

"Mhm, it's true. Selene was telling me all about it," Jimenez said with a laugh.

"S-Selene?" Fallon gave Javier a sideways glance.

"Yeah, my sister. She's one of Tegan's best friends," Jimenez said while absentmindedly scrolling through his phone.

"I thought Declan was Tegan's best friend." Fallon tapped his talons against the armrest of the sectional.

Jimenez shrugged and kept scrolling. "I don't know, man. They're all close. They have sleepovers and shit all the time. Well, at least they did before Atlas came into the picture."

"Trust me, they're still around all the time. But Tegan's friends are my friends. Whatever makes her happy." The tip of Atlas's tail wagged ever so slightly.

He was head over heels for my sister. I felt like a jackass for ever being opposed to it.

While everyone chatted, I nursed my virgin mojito and did whatever I could to keep from staring at Cyrus.

He looked so good with the last rays of sunlight shining off his smooth skin. His tentacles gently swayed as he spoke, like how you'd tap your fingers or bounce your leg, and each time Atlas told a joke or rehashed a funny story, he'd throw back his head with a laugh, like everything that came out of his friend's mouth was the funniest thing he'd ever heard.

"I, uh, I gotta take a piss," I said, setting my drink down and rising off the sectional with a groan.

"Oh, I can show—" Fallon started to say, but Cyrus cut him off.

"I'll show him where it is. I wanted to give Reece a little tour anyway."

"That would be great." I followed behind Cyrus.

We were both silent as we walked inside and down the hall to the bathroom. My body tingled with anticipation. Sitting across from Cyrus all night and not being able to touch him had been complete torture.

He came to a stop at the bathroom and leaned against the doorway while I walked inside. I watched as he tilted back, his finned head peeking down the hallway, making sure the coast was clear before he slipped inside.

I was on him the moment the lock clicked, pushing him against the door and kissing my way down the finned column of his neck.

"You're so fucking sexy, you know that?" I mumbled against his smooth skin while my hands slid over his back, down to where his torso ended and his tentacles began.

"Am not," he whispered, and gripped my chin, forcing me to make eye contact with him. "Especially compared to you, you sexy fucking tease."

His mating tentacle unraveled and massaged my cock through my shorts. It was the kraken equivalent to frotting, and I lived for every second of it.

I whimpered, thrusting my hips to meet his tentacle, and Cyrus let out a dark laugh.

"Darling, you know I love it when you're a needy boy, but we can't. Not with all these people here. Is this how you want them to find out? Them hearing us fucking in the bathroom?"

I sighed and pressed my forehead against his, staring into his wide eyes. "You're right. I'm just horny."

He snorted and slipped one of his hands underneath my shirt, the tips of his fingers gently caressing the outlines of my abs. "When are you not horny?"

"For you, never."

Cyrus smiled and pressed his lips to mine, but he didn't go further than that, a quick kiss and nothing more. "Now that you've had some attention, do you want to see the rest of the apartment? Fallon's room is a fucking mess as usual, but I can show you my room and the studio."

For as long as we'd been fooling around, I'd never been here. With Fallon as Cyrus's roommate, we kept things mostly contained to the gym or the odd evening at my place.

I wanted to see his space, but I was more interested in seeing his art. I'd asked him to send me pictures of what he was currently working on, but he was always so damn secretive about it.

"I'd like that."

I groaned when Cyrus pulled away, adjusting my boner and doing what I could to make it less visible.

"There really isn't a good way to hide that thing." He smiled and raised his eyebrows.

"Cheeky fuck."

"Cheeky? Look at that. Not only am I rubbing you off, I'm rubbing off on you." His fins vibrated with laughter.

"Are you going to show me around the fucking apartment or are you going to stand there and make fun of me?"

"Yes, yes. Come on. You're grouchy when you don't get your way, you know that?" He held the door open and when I went to pass him, he grabbed my shoulder. "Might just have to spank that bratty behavior right out of you next time, hmm?" he whispered against my ear.

I froze and closed my eyes. "Fuck."

"Come on then," he said and shuffled down the hallway. "We'll start with my room and then I'll show you the studio."

Cyrus's bedroom was exactly what I expected.

It was masculine and modern, with an exposed brick wall behind the bed, and bright white walls covered with moody oil paintings in varying tones of blue and green. A record player sat on a shelving unit filled to the brim with vinyl; an extensive collection of all the '80s sad boy shit Cyrus loved.

"Damn." I spun a globe that sat next to the record player. "I knew your room was going to put mine to shame."

It wasn't that I was messy or dirty; design just didn't come naturally to me like it did to Cyrus. I kept my furniture to the essentials, and I was clueless when it came to home decor.

"I like your place." Cyrus came up behind me, resting his head on my shoulder and wrapping his arms around my waist. "But I'm happy to help you spruce it up a bit if you'd like. In fact, I think I have some paintings in storage that would work well."

"You'd give me some of your art?"

Cyrus's work sold for thousands of dollars. He'd been featured in magazines and had gallery shows all over the world, and he wanted to give me some paintings?

"Mhm." He nuzzled his face against my neck. "And every time you walk past them, you'll be reminded of me."

"Cyrus, I—"

I had so many things I wanted to say. So many feelings —especially one feeling in particular—I wanted to express.

Feelings that were strange and foreign to me; that had my heart beating fast and gave me the warm fuzzies.

They were there, and they were for Cyrus, but they scared the shit out of me.

So I shoved them down.

Cyrus gripped my hand tight and kissed my cheek. It was like we were connected. Like he knew what I was feeling without me uttering a single word.

"Come on, darling. I'll show you the studio."

He popped his head out of the doorway, checking that it was just the two of us in the apartment before leading me to the studio, his hand still holding mine.

Because of his webbing, we struggled to thread our fingers together, but it never really bothered me. I was just happy to be touching him.

It was crazy what a difference a few months could make. How one being could change your whole outlook.

"Here we are," Cyrus said as he pushed open the door.

"Shit," I muttered under my breath, and stepped inside the studio.

It was gorgeous.

Large windows lined one of the walls and against the other was a row of canvases. Some were covered with drop cloths, but there were a few completed paintings out on display.

Cyrus leaned against a workbench covered with paints and brushes, and I headed straight for the paintings. They were mostly landscapes: forest scenes, coastal towns, and even a few places around Briar Glenn I recognized.

"Cyrus, these are beautiful," I said, glancing over at him. His arms were crossed over his broad chest, a shy smile turning up the corner of his lips, but I could tell he was beaming with pride.

"I'm glad you like them," he said as he shuffled over next to me. "For the first time in a long time, I'm feeling inspired." He reached down and grabbed my hand, the two of us staring at the canvases. "You crashed into my life when I least expected it, but also when I needed it most. You can be a dickhead, but you're *my* dickhead. My life is infinitely better with you in it, Reece Rollins."

My cheeks flushed and tears formed in the corners of my eyes when Cyrus brought my hand up to his lips.

"Come on," he said quietly. "We should get back to the party."

"Wait." I stepped in front of him.

I held his face between my hands and pressed my lips to his, kissing him like my life depended on it, using my actions to say what I couldn't admit to.

At least not yet.

Because my life was infinitely better with him in it too.

NINETEEN

Cyrus

"Good morning," Reece said with a smile as he slid into the passenger seat. He leaned over the center console and kissed me, the wiry hairs of his beard and mustache tickling my face.

"Good morning, *indeed*," I said as he fastened his seat-belt. "How are we feeling about today?" I asked, putting the car in park and starting off toward the lake.

"I'm not gonna lie. I'm nervous. But I watched some videos on ankle flexion, doubled up on my electrolytes, and I've been exclusively taking cold showers, so I should be set."

Today he'd be doing another open water swim. After nearly drowning the last time he'd attempted it, I knew he'd be nervous, but I had something up my sleeve that would help.

"Confident and relaxed. Love to see it."

Reece slid his free hand into mine as he scrolled through his phone with the other. "So, you'll be at dinner tomorrow, right?"

A few of us had been invited to Atlas and Tegan's for

dinner tomorrow, for what we assumed was some sort of wedding party formation. Reece and Tegan had been getting along better as of late, but he was still wary about the strength of their relationship.

Gods, he was fucking cute.

Underneath that tough exterior, he was a sensitive teddy bear, especially when it came to his younger sister.

I smiled and shook my head, using one of my tentacles to nudge his leg. "Yes, I've told you how many times already? I'll be there. I was thinking that maybe after you could spend the night at my place? Fallon mentioned he and Jimenez are going to the club after. We'll have the apartment all to ourselves."

"Fuckkk," he groaned. "You better fuck me in that tub."

"I'll fuck you anywhere you want, darling. Just say the word."

"Darling," he said and leaned his head against the window, refusing to look at me. "I like it when you call me that."

I'd bet money he was blushing.

"Good, because I don't intend to stop."

I pulled the car into the empty parking lot at the lake and we both got out.

"Gods, this was a poor choice," Reece hissed as he pulled his hoodie up around his neck. "I'm never doing a tri in the fall again."

I laughed and popped open my trunk, pulling out a garment bag and holding it up for Reece to see. "Well, that's a shame, considering you have one of these now."

Reece smiled wide and eagerly opened the bag. "You didn't. A wetsuit. Cy, these things aren't fucking cheap."

"I know you were planning to buy one closer to the race, but I wanted you to have it. Consider it a gift from trainer to student. I guessed on the size a bit, but I wanted it to be a surprise. Hopefully, it fits."

Reece launched himself at me, throwing his arms around my neck and smacking his lips against mine. If it weren't for my tentacles catching us, we would have toppled over onto the asphalt.

"I'll have to give you gifts more often. Speaking of, has your present arrived yet?" I wiggled my eyebrows at him. Well, as best as I could wiggle the bumpy crests above my eyes.

He bit his lip and nodded his head.

"Did you use it yet?" I whispered.

Reece shook his head no.

"When you do, I want you to video chat with me. I want to see your face while you fuck it and think of me. Will you do that for me?" I purred against his throat.

"Y-Yes. Whatever you want." His voice was practically a whine.

I loved teasing him, loved knowing that my mate yearned for me and wanted to please me.

"That's my good boy. Now, let's see if we can get this thing on. Oh, wait. I almost forgot." I pulled a bag from the trunk and handed it to Reece.

With a confused look, he pulled a spray canister out of the bag. "Is this cooking spray?"

"No," I snorted. "It's some fancy spray lube. It prevents chafing and it's supposed to help with getting your wetsuit on."

He grinned at me and my hearts raced.

"Thank you, Cy. I don't know what I would do without you."

My tentacles clenched tight to my arms and I could feel my face flushing a darker blue. "I want you to do well and I know this is important to you. Now come on, let's see how long it takes us to get this thing on."

Reece and I walked side by side over to the changing stalls at the start of the beach. They were all empty, because as usual, we were the only ones here at the lake on a cool morning.

We crammed inside the stall and Reece immediately began to undress.

"Motherfucker," he groaned as he pulled his hoodie over his head. His light pink nipples pebbled in the cool morning air, and I had to suppress the urge to pop one into my mouth.

We were here with a purpose, and that purpose wasn't to fuck in a confined space.

We did that enough at the gym.

"Alright, then," I said when Reece was undressed down to his jammers. "Let me lube you up."

He put his hands on his hips and laughed. "Can you not say that? The last thing I need is to get a boner while we're trying to get this on."

"What?" I said as I sprayed his ankles and calves with the lube. "It isn't my fault you find me irresistible. Legs up."

Reece wriggled one foot into the wetsuit and then the other.

"Okay, not too bad." I used my tentacles to pull the tight neoprene over his calves. "Your thighs are going to be the real challenge, though. You could crush a watermelon with these things."

Reece chuckled and wiggled his hips as we worked the material over his thighs with slow tugs.

"Goddess is this thing fucking tight." I dramatically wiped my brow with one of my tentacles.

"Will you stop fucking making me laugh." His body

shook with laughter as I continued to wrench the wetsuit over it. "We're trying to do something serious and suddenly you turn into a fucking comedian."

I reached the bulge at Reece's crotch and absolutely lost it, bursting into a fit of laughter that had my fins vibrating along my neck.

"Reece!" I huffed. "Control yourself. And here you are giving me shit."

He blushed and held out his hands. "You were rubbing all over me! I'm sorry. It happens."

This was the Reece Rollins I loved. The Reece Rollins so few people got to see.

"Come on, we're almost there." I sprayed his wrists and around his neck with lube.

"Wait." Reece held his hand out. "Let me see that."

I passed him the lube and he sprayed both of his nipples until the pointed tips glistened.

"Don't want any chafing."

"Oh, good thinking, darling. I knew you were more than just a pretty face."

"Will you stop fucking around and help me," he said as he shimmied his arms into the wetsuit.

"Alright, alright." I rose on my tentacles and gripped the back of the suit, pulling it over the broad expanse of Reece's back. "How's that?" I asked when I finished pulling up the zipper.

I stepped back, giving Reece space while he flexed his arms and shook out his legs.

"I think it's perfect. You got the sizing spot on."

I stared at his crotch, squinting my eyes as I leaned in closer. "I don't know. I think you could have used a bigger size here. I wonder if there's a cut for men with big dicks."

"You're such a horny fuck, you know that?" he said as he stepped past me and out of the changing stall.

"Oh, I know, and you love every minute of it."

"Pfft," he huffed as he stomped toward the beach. Even with his back turned to me, I knew he was smiling.

I was definitely a horny fuck because I followed behind him just far enough away that I could watch the cheeks of his ass flex underneath the wetsuit.

Gods, I couldn't wait to fuck him later.

He put on his swim cap and goggles, and I watched as he did his stretches. When he was finally warmed up, he walked over to me.

"For good luck." Reece pressed his lips against mine in a quick kiss.

One of my tentacles snaked around his waist, pulling him closer so we were pressed chest to chest.

"You're going to do great. I know it." My tentacle gave his ass a light swat. "Now get in the water."

He pulled away from me and rushed toward the lake, diving underneath the water the moment it was deep enough. I tapped my phone and started the timer, watching as Reece began to swim with powerful strokes.

I was nervous, and though I'd offered to join him in the water, he'd insisted on doing this on his own, driving home the fact that on race day I'd have to watch him from the shore.

His form was perfection. Not only was the wetsuit keeping him warm, but it was helping with drag and buoyancy. I looked down at my phone as he reached the halfway marker and was shocked.

This was his best time yet—and in an open water swim.

"Yes, Reece!" I shouted from the beach as he reached the far buoy and switched direction. I wasn't sure if he could hear me, but I wasn't going to speak to him in his head and potentially distract him.

As he got closer to the shore, I scuttled out into the shallow water, ready to congratulate my mate.

"How did I do?" he asked as he rose out of the water, trudging toward me with heavy breaths.

I stopped the timer and rushed forward, almost tackling him as I wrapped my arms around him.

"That was your best time yet."

"Are you shitting me?" He smiled wide as water dripped down his face and collected in his beard.

"No, look." He pulled his goggles up onto his head and I held up my phone for him to see.

"Yes!" he whooped and gripped me in another tight hug.

"You've got this in the bag. I am so proud of you."

Reece buried his face against my neck. "Thank you, Cy. Thank you for everything," he mumbled, his cool lips brushing against my skin with each word. "I couldn't have done this without you."

"You could have, your time just wouldn't have been as good."

"Fuck you," he said with a laugh and nuzzled against me.

But I knew what he was really trying to say, because I felt it too.

TWENTY

Reece

I flipped down my visor and looked in the mirror, brushing my hands over my beard and smoothing back my hair. It was bordering on too long, but I knew Cyrus liked it. I guess when you had zero hair to speak of, it was fascinating being with someone who had it. I was even contemplating growing out my chest hair for him.

The things that kraken could get me to do.

My phone vibrated in my cup holder.

Cyrus: Are you going to come inside or are you going to sit there checking yourself out for another 15 minutes?

I glanced out the window, and sure enough, there was Cyrus, watching me from inside my sister's cottage.

Reece: Fucking creep. I'm coming.

Every time I was around Tegan, I was on edge. I was so afraid of doing or saying the wrong thing. Of upsetting her or Atlas. I wanted Tegan to know that I was better—that I was working on myself—that I'd changed.

Because I had.

I could tell from my interactions with monsters around town, and from the way I chatted with Atlas and Fallon. I genuinely enjoyed being around them, even if the griffon could be a little annoying.

My relationship with Cyrus was also proof I'd changed, but I wasn't ready to make things public yet. I didn't want it to seem like I was seeing him just to get in Atlas and Tegan's good graces.

What we had felt like something real, and it was special to me. I didn't want to risk fucking things up with him.

My phone vibrated again.

Cyrus: No, that's later *wink face emoji*

Cyrus always had this way of making me feel at ease, of breaking any tension I was feeling. Whether it was with humor or a soft touch, it was one of the things I appreciated most about him. He knew how to reach parts of me that no one else could.

That applied to the tentacles too.

There was a knock on the window and I almost jumped out of my skin.

"Honey, what are you doing just sitting out here?" my mother asked from outside the car.

Goddess help me.

"Hey, Ma," I said as I stepped out of the car. "I was just catching up on a few emails real quick."

I leaned over and wrapped her in a tight hug before pulling away.

She looked me up and down. "Well, don't you look handsome."

I could feel my cheeks turning red, so I stared down at my outfit.

Yeah, I wanted to look nice for whatever wedding formality this was, but I *really* wanted to look nice for Cyrus and our plans later.

"Do you need help bringing anything inside?"

"Nope, Atlas and Tegan insisted I didn't bring anything. You know how stubborn your sister can be." She threw up her arms in a shrug and we walked to the front door.

Of course I knew how stubborn my sister could be, because I was the same fucking way.

Before we could knock on the front door, it swung open and Atlas greeted us with a sharp-toothed smile.

"Hey there, Mrs. Rollins." He bent over to hug my mom. The two of them were comical together since she was even smaller than my sister.

"Atlas!" She swatted his chest playfully. "What did I tell you about that? It's either mom or Pam. None of that Mrs. Rollins nonsense."

Gods, the woman was a trip.

"Reece." Atlas held out his arms and I braced myself for impact.

Yep, he was still a strong motherfucker. Maybe it was some sort of dominance thing with wolven males—whoever could give the most crushing hug was the top dog.

We stepped inside the cottage to find everyone relaxing in the living area.

"Damn, it looks great in here," I said as my eyes scanned the interior.

Even since the barbecue, Atlas had done so much work to the place that I barely recognized it.

"Doesn't it?" My sister beamed as she stepped out from behind the kitchen island and made her way over to us. "Atlas has been working overtime." Tegan hugged our mother, then turned to me.

"Hi, big brother," she said as she wrapped her arms around me. "You look nice." She took a deep inhale against my chest. "And you smell nice too. What is that, cologne?"

I rubbed my hand along the back of my neck and shrugged. "Figured it was a special occasion, might as well."

"Special occasion, indeed," Cyrus said from the couch. Tegan's friend Declan sat on one side of him and Selene sat on the other.

"Where are Jimenez—I mean Javier—and Fallon?" I asked as I sat down at the island next to my mother.

"Fallon said Javi was picking him up because they're going to the club later. They're probably just running a bit late. Let me send Fallon a text," Cyrus said, picking up his phone.

"Figures." Selene sighed and rubbed her temples.

"Well, uh, while we wait for them, you guys can have some appetizers. Reece, would you mind helping me set the table on the deck? I thought that since it's so nice out we could eat outside." My sister stared at me with expectant green eyes that were identical to my own.

"Y-Yeah, of course." I glanced over at Cyrus and he smiled.

"Thanks." Tegan passed me a heavy stack of plates topped with rolls of silverware.

"Honey, do you need help—" our mother started as we headed toward the slider that led to the deck.

"We've got it, Mom," Tegan said as she closed the door behind us.

I sat the plates down on the table and quietly prepped the place settings while Tegan stared at me with her hands on her hips.

"Reece, um. I was hoping we could talk for a bit. Just the two of us."

"Yeah, uh, sure. You wanna go somewhere, or...?"

"I have some lawn chairs set up in the yard. Let's go out there."

I followed behind her as she led us to a pair of chairs placed right along the treeline. We both sat, and for a while we were quiet, the silence filled by the sound of swaying leaves and the last songs of the summer crickets.

"You probably know why everyone is here, right?" Tegan finally said and tucked a few stray hairs from her bun behind her ear.

I shrugged. "I mean, I figured it has something to do with the wedding party."

She nodded her head. "It does. But, I—I wanted to ask you something. You specifically."

Tegan turned towards me, her face scrunched up with a squint due to the afternoon sun. She reminded me of how she'd looked when we were kids. When we were still close.

"Since Dad's gone, I wanted to know if you'd walk me down the aisle and give me away." She reached over and held my hand for the first time in who knew how long. "I know you've been working on yourself, and it shows in the way you interact with Atlas and his friends. And honestly,

Reece, you seem different. Lighter. Happier. I don't know how to explain it, but a few people have noticed it. I'm proud of how much you've grown, and I love you. This is going to be a special day for me, and I want you to be a part of it."

I felt like I was going to cry.

I mean, I wouldn't, at least not right now, but I was touched.

"I love you, and I couldn't have picked a more perfect mate for you than Atlas. I'd be honored to walk you down the aisle and give you away."

I meant it, too. Every single word.

Tegan sprang up to hug me, nearly falling out of her chair in the process.

"Thank you for asking me," I mumbled against her hair as she held me tight.

"Of course. You're the only one it could have been. I just didn't want to put you on the spot in front of everyone." She pulled away and wiped underneath her eyes.

Was she crying?

I guess Tegan had missed me just as much as I missed her.

"Hey." I grabbed her arm. "None of that. This is a happy day. I'm assuming everyone else in there is a part of the wedding too?"

She nodded her head.

"I can't have them thinking I made you upset," I said with a smile, and Tegan laughed.

"They're happy tears, Reecie."

"Come on." I rose from my seat with a groan and held my hand out to Tegan. "Let's get this table set so we can eat. I'm starving."

After we finished setting the table, Atlas carried out big trays of salad and baked ziti.

"She seems happy. You said yes?" he asked as he peeled back the aluminum foil covering the trays.

"Of course I did."

The wolven smiled wide and gripped my shoulder with one of his massive paws. "I knew you would. You're a good guy, Reece. I'm happy you're going to be my brother-in-law."

"I'm happy you're going to be my brother-in-law too, but we need to talk about the hugs." I rubbed my chest dramatically and Atlas barked out a laugh.

"I'll work on it." He lowered his voice to a gravelly whisper. "Speaking of hugs, are you, uh, seeing anyone?" Atlas stared through the slider to where the rest of the group was gathered.

"N-No," I stammered.

Gods, I was shit at this.

Atlas didn't drop it, though. "I was going for a run the other morning and I could have sworn I saw you with someone down by the lake."

"It was probably just me and Cyrus training."

He tilted his head to stare at me and his tail swayed back and forth slightly. "Mmm, I'm pretty sure this was more than just training."

My stomach dropped and my heart raced.

"Hey." Atlas gripped my shoulders. "Hey. It's okay. It's fine. You're consenting adults. I was just asking because Cyrus seems to be doing a lot better. Before he started training you, Fallon and I were a little worried about him. I don't want to put his business out there, but he was pretty depressed."

It took a moment for what he said to register.

"Cyrus was depressed before he met me?"

"Mhm." Atlas nodded.

"Does anyone else know?"

"Do you really think I'd do that to one of my best friends and my future brother-in-law? I haven't said a word. And I won't. If—*when*—you guys are ready to go public with things, you one-hundred percent have my support."

The sliding door flew open and Fallon rushed outside.

"Atlas, I need to talk to you about something!" the griffon chirped with his feathers ruffled up around his neck and his tail swishing in agitation.

"Can it wait until after dinner?" Atlas asked.

"I don't know, man. I'm having a crisis here." Fallon closed his beady eyes and threw back his head, taking a deep breath.

That was my cue.

"I'll, uh, leave you two to it, then," I said and slipped back inside the house.

"Ey, boss man!" Jimenez's voice tore through the living area the moment I stepped into the house. "I heard you're going to be walking your sister down the aisle."

I smiled. "Yep, and I'm damn proud of it."

"I can't believe my baby is getting married." My mom wrapped her arm around Tegan, putting her head on my sister's shoulder.

"She's going to be the most beautiful bride, Mrs. R." Declan raised his wine glass and took a long drink.

I wondered how long it would take for dinner to devolve into all the single parties heading out to the bar or the club. Hopefully not too long, because I was dying to have Cyrus's place all to ourselves.

Atlas popped his head through the sliding door. "We're all ready out here!"

"I wasn't finished yet," Fallon squawked.

"Shh," Atlas growled, shutting him up.

"Well." Tegan rose to her feet. "Let's eat."

We headed outside, joining Atlas and Fallon at the table.

Everyone slipped into their chairs, with Selene sitting as far away from Fallon as possible.

"This seat taken?" I asked, standing next to where Cyrus sat.

"Nope. Have a seat."

Cyrus's accent combined with his soft smirk almost put me over the edge.

I needed to get myself under control. Atlas was already onto us and I wasn't ready for anyone else to know yet.

Atlas cleared his throat from where he sat at the head of the table. "Tegan and I appreciate all of you joining us today. As you've probably already guessed, we'd like to ask each of you to play a part in our special day."

Tegan reached over and gripped Atlas's massive hand. "You've all heard that Reece has agreed to give me away at the ceremony." Cheers came from around the table and Tegan smiled sweetly at Selene. "Selene, I was wondering if you'd be my maid of honor?"

Selene grinned at Tegan. "It would be my pleasure."

"Dec." Tegan looked across the table at Declan. "Will you be my bridesman?"

"Teg, I will be whatever you need me to be."

"And of course, you'll be the matron of honor, Mom."

"Oh, honey. I can't wait." Ma fanned her eyes, on the verge of tears.

Atlas looked at Fallon, giving the griffon a knowing smile. "While I do love my brothers, they live across the country. They'll be coming to the wedding, but it just didn't feel right asking one of them to be my best man. Fal, you're my oldest friend. Would you do me the honor of being my best man?"

"A-man, I'd love to. I'm going to throw you a killer bachelor party," Fallon chuffed.

"Cy, you're my second oldest friend, and I'll need someone to keep Fallon in check. Will you be one of my groomsmen?" Atlas stared down the table at Cyrus.

"I'd be honored to. I'll do my best with Fallon, but no promises."

The three of them had such a tight friendship, and despite the fact that I was originally an asshole, they'd accepted me into their circle with open arms.

"Uh, what about Jim—I mean, Javier?" I asked, realizing his role in the wedding hadn't been established.

"Oh, Tegan asked me to be the officiant. I got a certificate online." Jimenez raised his chin at me and smirked.

"Well, with that settled, let's eat." Atlas sat down and scooped a generous serving of ziti onto his plate.

While everyone talked and ate, I slid my foot over until it tapped Cyrus's tentacles. One of the long appendages coiled around my ankle, gripping it softly while he continued his conversation with Jimenez.

There I was, sharing a meal with monsters.

I wasn't scared of them anymore.

I cared about all the beings at this table—but the monster sitting next to me was the most important one of all.

TWENTY-ONE

Cyrus

My tentacles shuffled over the carpet, propelling me down the hallway and back again.

Why in the goddesses name was I so nervous?

It wasn't like this was the first time Reece had been over to my place. It was just the first time the two of us would be here, *alone*, in my apartment.

Free to do as we pleased, wherever we pleased.

A gentle knock echoed down the hall and I did my best not to bolt toward the door. Well, I couldn't exactly bolt, so I did my best not to rush to the door, indicating I'd been impatiently waiting in the hallway for Reece to arrive.

"Hi," Reece said.

"Hi."

We stood there for a second, just staring at one another, when my tentacles grabbed him and pulled him inside.

"Fuck," he groaned as I pinned him against the wall. "I have been dying to touch you all night."

I laughed and slid my lips over his neck while I rolled my hips against his. "It was torture. And when you sat down next to me, what was that about?"

"You're not the only one that's a tease."

His breath hitched as one of my mating tentacles unraveled and massaged his cock. "Mmm, my sexy little tease. Already so hard for me. What do you want to do first? If you're hungry we can—"

"Cyrus, I swear to the gods if you don't get inside me soon I'm going to come in my pants. Tonight was nonstop edging."

I gave him a quick kiss and pulled away. "Alright. Hold your horses. I'll get you off. Do you want to take a bath together first?"

Ever since I'd sent Reece a series of photos of me taking a bath, he'd been obsessed with the idea of us fucking in my soaking tub.

"Gods yes!" he blurted and immediately started kicking off his shoes.

"Control yourself, darling. We have all night. Grab your shoes and undress in my room. I don't want your clothes all over the place when Fallon comes home. And where did you park your car?"

I was hopeful that Fallon would spend the night with one of his conquests or end up passed out at Javier's house, but on the off chance he did come home, I wanted it to appear like I was alone. Reece could quietly slip out in the morning and all would be well in the world.

"Don't worry, I hid it around the block. And it's Fallon we're talking about, do you really think he'd notice my car in the parking lot?"

I shrugged and started down the hallway with Reece following behind me. "You never know. I'm just trying to keep this as quiet for you as I can."

We walked into the bathroom and Reece was silent as I

grabbed fresh towels, no longer showing the enthusiasm he'd had out in the hall.

"Is something wrong?" I asked and scuttled toward him, my tentacles popping along the tile as I went.

His face flamed red and he rubbed his hand along the back of his neck. "At the party. Atlas, um, he stopped me outside. He knows about us. He saw us together down at the lake."

Reece leaned against the vanity and I stood beside him. Reaching over, I took his hand while my tentacle wrapped around his arm.

"Did he tell anyone?" I asked, keeping my voice calm and quiet.

Reece shook his head.

"How do you feel about that? I know you wanted to tell everyone on your own terms and I respect that."

He scrubbed his free hand over the wiry, red strands of his beard. "I mean, I guess out of all the people to find out, Atlas is the best one. Better him than Fallon. But I thought for sure we were being careful. I'd never ask you to keep this a secret forever, Cy. I just..."

"Hey." I stepped in front of him. "It's okay to be upset about this. You're allowed to feel that way." I grabbed his other hand and pressed my forehead against his. "And I know you'd never keep us a secret forever, but you're allowed to take as long as you need to process things. Atlas is as loyal and trustworthy as they come. When you're ready, he'll be there to support us. He won't say a single thing before then."

Reece tightened his grip on my hands. "You're right. I'm happy, but I'm afraid of ruining it."

Knowing my mate was happy had me practically bursting with pride. "Reece, nothing could ever ruin this."

There was a small part of me that had my doubts, though. I had this lingering fear that as soon as we went public with our relationship, or as soon as I told Reece about the mate bond, he'd backslide and regret everything between us.

I'd be crushed.

That was a worry for another day, though.

Tonight, I wanted to enjoy him, to enjoy *us*.

I dipped my head, pressed my lips to his, and with a low groan I slid the soft pads of my tongues into his mouth, swirling and teasing until Reece lightly bucked his hips into mine, searching for friction.

I released his hands and pulled away, slipping down his body until the bulge in his pants was level with my mouth.

"How many times do you think I can make you come tonight?" I asked, tilting my head back to stare into his eyes as I slowly undid his belt.

"Over and over, until I pass out, preferably." He reached for his waistband, but my tentacles darted out, restraining his hands behind his back.

"Someone's impatient," I said with a smirk. "You stay put, darling. I'll give you what you need."

With steady hands, I started to pull his shorts down.

"What. Is. This." I gasped at the sight of the thin black lace that strained against the impressive length of Reece's cock. Skinny straps on the sides dug into his hips just slightly before disappearing between the cheeks of his ass.

I knew full well what it was, but I wanted my mate to say it.

His cheeks flushed beet red. "I-it's a thong. This was part of a dream I had. A dream about you," he mumbled under his breath.

"Mmm," I purred and nuzzled my face against the

material. *Against Reece's cock.* "If this is part of the dream, you'll have to fill me in on the rest of it."

It turned out my straight-laced mate was kinkier than I'd thought. I wanted to please him, to live out every fantasy his deliciously dirty mind could come up with.

"In fact," I said as I pulled the thong to the side, allowing Reece's cock to drop free. "Why don't you tell me the details of this dream while I suck you off? Hmm?"

I placed a delicate kiss on the tip of his head, smearing the bead of precum that had collected there over my lips. My tongues darted out to lick it, and I hummed with satisfaction at the flavor.

Reece swallowed hard, his breaths coming out as harsh pants while he stared down at me.

I was a hair's breadth away from his cock. It would take nothing to open my mouth and slip him inside, but I wanted him to answer me first.

I wanted him to tell me about the dream.

Just when I started to pull back, Reece spoke. "You were degrading me. You were asking me how much I liked it. You said it was the tentacles. That it's always the tentacles..."

I parted my lips and slid the smooth head of Reece's cock into my mouth.

"Shit," he hissed through clenched teeth, his hips thrusting slightly and his arms straining against my tentacles. Reece was strong, but my mate was no match for the restraints.

Go on, I told him using my telepathic abilities while I held his cock still in my mouth, refusing to take him deeper until he told me more of the dream.

"One of your tentacles slid around my throat and

choked me. Not too hard, just a little bit. Just enough to make breathing tough."

Oh? Do you like that sort of thing?

My eyes were fixed on Reece's fevered expression as I bobbed my head, using my tongues to caress the wide vein running along the top of his cock.

"Y-yes. I think so." He groaned through parted lips and threw his head back. "I-I've never done it before."

Would you like to try it?

Consent was key, and I never wanted to do anything to Reece that made him feel uncomfortable. Especially something like breath play. You had to have trust.

I moved my head faster, taking the tip of his cock into the back of my throat while my tongues coiled around the shaft.

"Fuck. Yes. Please," he said through gritted teeth.

My tentacle traced up his body before wrapping around his neck, slowly increasing the pressure along the sides of his throat.

How's that?

"Amazing," he rasped against the soft squeeze.

"Good."

He gasped as I plunged the full length of his cock into my mouth.

Unlike humans, I didn't have a gag reflex. I could take his cock into my throat as far as it would go.

And I did.

Over and over again.

"Holy shit, Cyrus," Reece huffed as he thrust his hips to meet my mouth.

What else happened in the dream?

"I-I begged you to fuck me. You gave me your suckers.

You played with my prostate. We both came hard and you told me how well I did." He was trying to focus but his words came out in a rushed string.

It appeared that my mate, the muscle-head parks worker triathlete, was into lace thongs, praise, and degradation.

How did I get so lucky?

"Cyrus," he panted. "Gonna come."

Give it to me, darling. Come in the back of my throat. Let me taste you.

I forced him deeper into my throat, his hips slamming against my face as he filled my mouth with his cum. The salty flavor was exquisite, and I used my tongues to work every last drop out of his cock.

"Motherfucker," he groaned as his body convulsed against the restraints.

I pulled away just slightly, allowing my tongues to swirl over his shaft several times before I popped off of his cock.

"Was it good?" I asked, staring up at him expectantly.

I knew the answer was yes, but again, I needed my mate to say it. I needed verbal confirmation that my dual-tongued blowjobs were the most superior in all the land.

His eyes were hooded and his chest heaved as he looked down at me. "You are the king of blow jobs, Cy."

"Damn right, I am."

My tentacles released Reece and I rose to a standing position next to him.

"How about that bath now, hmm?" I asked, skating my hands under his shirt, along his cut six pack.

"Please." Reece circled his arms around my neck, pulling me in for a kiss.

He slipped his tongue past my lips, claiming my mouth with possessive strokes. Apparently, it didn't bother him that he'd just filled my mouth with his cum.

"I love how fucking filthy you are," I mumbled.

He laughed as I pulled away. "There are worse things than tasting my own cum."

I shuffled over to the tub, starting the tap while Reece undressed. Since he'd be joining me, I didn't add my usual salt crystals, opting for a lightly scented bubble bath instead.

As I was bent over the tub, using my tentacles to agitate the water, I felt the warmth of Reece's nude body press up against me. Strong hands wrapped around my chest and he nestled his face against my fins.

"I just can't get enough of you," he whispered. "You looked so handsome. So focused. I had to touch you."

Months ago, Reece would have shied away from touching me, now he actively sought me out.

A wide smile spread over my face, and I ran the backside of my hand along his beard, right where the stubble ended and the smooth column of his neck began.

How was it that someone ripped from the pages of *Men's Health* magazine found me attractive?

It had to be because of the mate bond. That was the only explanation. There was no way I could pull a guy like Reece otherwise.

"Everything okay?" he asked when I didn't respond to his compliment.

"Everything's fine. Better than fine, actually." I looked down at the bubbling water line of the tub. "We can get in now if you'd like. It can fill up the rest of the way with us in there."

He nodded, releasing me so that I could slide over the side and into the bath.

I hummed as the warm water blanketed my body and held my hand out to help Reece. He stepped in, settling himself next to me in our bubble fortress.

"This is really nice," he said, collecting a wad of bubbles in his hand, then blowing them into the tub.

While I called it a soaking tub, it was more like a jacuzzi or hot tub, with ample room for two grown men to lie comfortably.

"Come here." I braced myself against the side of the tub, using my tentacles to pull Reece against me.

"This is even better," he mumbled, snuggling closer, and pressing his ear to my chest.

We sat like that for a few moments, enjoying the close-ness of one another as the tub filled.

"Cy," Reece said the moment I shut off the tap.

"Yes, darling?"

"Your heartbeat. It's sort of weird." He rubbed his hand over my chest, feeling my thumping hearts underneath.

"That's because I have three hearts."

And they all beat for you.

He stared up at me, a light coating of bubbles stuck to his beard. "Really?"

"Really."

"Wild."

Reece wiggled against me, and I could feel his hard-ening cock poking my tentacles.

"Already?" I asked with a laugh.

The needy thing had just gotten off.

"I can't help it." He rubbed his hands over my chest, continuing upward until his fingertips trailed over my fins. "You turn me on. And you did promise me you'd fuck me in this bathtub."

"Well, I can't break a promise. Sit up for me."

Reece sat sideways in my lap, his back braced against the tub wall and his feet propped against the opposite ledge. He sat just high enough that the head of his cock jutted out from the water's surface, giving me the perfect view.

"You're going to stay still for me." My tentacles coiled around Reece's arms, pinning them behind his back.

"Fuck," he murmured as one of my tentacles curled around the base of his cock.

"Spread your legs," I instructed, my voice flat.

He complied but didn't spread his legs nearly as far apart as I wanted them.

With one hand, I gripped his thigh, forcing his legs wider and sending water sloshing over the edge of the tub.

"Shit, Cy," he panted.

Apparently, Reece liked it rough.

My mating tentacles uncoiled from my arms, the tips already coated in a light sheen of lubricant.

"Open your mouth," I commanded.

If he wanted breath play, I'd give it to him, and get myself off at the same time.

Reece parted his full lips and I slid my mating tentacle into his mouth. With quick thrusts, I worked the slick tendril into the back of his throat as he gagged around it.

"Take it, my needy boy. I'm going to fill all of your holes. Leave you dripping with my cum like the little cum slut you are."

Degradation wasn't normally my thing, but if Reece was into it, I was willing to do a bit of role-playing.

Beneath the water, my other mating tentacle slid over his ass and circled his entrance, coating the area with lube. This was one of the perks of being a kraken, I was designed for sex in the water.

"Are you ready, darling? Ready to be stuffed with my tentacles?" I asked.

He let out a muffled groan as I slowly pushed the tip inside, giving his body time to adjust to the stretch.

I stared at him and smirked, reveling in the fact that I could reduce this hyper-masculine man into a desperate, whimpering mess.

He was so damn pretty like this.

Saliva dripped down his chin, his eyes watering as I continued fucking his mouth. My tentacle stroked his cock, gripping and twisting his shaft, distracting him as the tentacle in his ass burrowed deeper.

It wasn't enough though.

I knew my mate.

He needed more.

Another one of my tentacles slid out of the water, over his stomach, and up his chest, coming to a stop at one of his nipples.

"These sexy pecs," I growled.

The tip of my tentacle curled around his nipple, giving it a sharp pinch.

"*Fuh,*" Reece mumbled against my tentacle, his body jolting against the restraints.

"Do you want to come?" I asked.

He gave me a slow nod.

The mating tentacle in his ass forced itself deeper, pushing the rows of suckers past the tight ring of muscle.

"Gods damn, Reece," I groaned, enjoying the sensation just as much as he did.

With both of my mating tentacles being stimulated, I was close to coming myself.

The suckers coating the underside of my tentacle found his prostate, massaging the gland with rapid passes before attaching.

"*Cy*," he moaned around my tentacle, his body quivering as he came.

"Yes, yes," I rasped, my gaze focused on his cock as thick spurts of cum coated his chest.

Warmth spread along my mating tentacles as I found my own release, flooding Reece's mouth and tight channel with my cum.

His Adam's apple bobbed with each of his desperate swallows, and a small stream of my cum trickled out of the corner of his mouth.

Slowly, I pulled out of him, savoring his contented expression as I wiped the cum off of his face.

"You did so well, taking all of my cum like that," I praised.

Reece groaned and threw his head back. "You fucking wrecked me, Cy."

I laughed and used my tentacle to pull the stopper, draining the bath. "You said you wanted me to fuck you in the tub. I wanted the first time to be memorable."

"Oh, it's fucking memorable alright. I'm gonna be walking funny tomorrow."

"Shut up," I said, pulling him closer and pressing my lips to his.

"Maybe not, but my nipple is going to be sore for sure."

"Well, I guess I'll just have to kiss it better then, won't I?" I smirked before rising up on my tentacles. "Come on, let's rinse off in the shower and get to bed."

TWENTY-TWO

Reece

"What's wrong?" Cyrus asked as I rolled over for what felt like the hundredth time.

His bed was comfortable, and obviously I enjoyed his company, but even after back-to-back orgasms, I just couldn't get my thoughts to stop racing.

"I'm just—feeling a little anxious."

Cyrus shimmied next to me so that my back was pressed against his chest, and wrapped one of his arms around me. "Talk to me, darling," he whispered.

"I just have a lot on my mind. The triathlon is coming up. The fact that Atlas saw us. My sister asking me to give her away."

"Well," he said, and rubbed his thumb over my stomach with slow strokes. "You've been busting your ass in training and you're going to do amazing in the triathlon. While there are worse things than Atlas finding out, it's okay to be upset that it wasn't on your terms. And your sister asking you to give her away—that's such a huge step forward in your relationship. You've come so far in the last three months, Reece. It's normal to have mixed feelings about that or worry that you're going to do something to screw it all up. But you're doing wonderful, darling. Sure, there might be setbacks, you might not place as well as you want to, and you might piss your sister off again at some point. No, not might, *will*. But you're out here giving it your all, regardless of what the final outcome is. I'm proud of you for that."

Cyrus was right. This was all part of change—of growth. It was going to be uncomfortable. I was going to have moments where I doubted myself or doubted the process, but I was giving it my all. That's what mattered.

And the fact that Cyrus was proud of me, that was an added bonus.

Cyrus pulled away from me and sat up. "Lie on your back. I want to try something."

I snorted and rolled onto my back. "Holy gods, Cy. You really want to fuck again? I don't know if my ass can take any more."

He laughed and pulled the sheet down off of my waist, revealing my soft cock. "No more fucking, at least not yet. Have you ever heard of cockwarming?"

"I mean, yeah. I've heard of it. I've never done it or had it done to me."

"Would you want to try it? I think it might help you relax a little bit. Just until you fall asleep, and you can still talk to me while I do it. If you don't like it, we can stop."

Having a—*friend*—with telepathic abilities had its advantages, and I did enjoy intimate touches when it came to Cyrus.

"Sure." I put my arms behind my head. "But I swear to the gods if you fall asleep and chomp off my cock with those piranha teeth, I will be pissed."

He laughed and slid down my body before slipping my cock between his soft lips. There wasn't any head bobbing, or lip and tongue action, he laid his head against my pelvis and held my limp cock in his mouth.

And it felt amazing.

Like a warm hug for my dick.

For the record, I'd never chomp off this absolute piece of perfection. Do you like it?

His sexy British accent echoed inside of my head and I couldn't help but smile. "Yeah. It's different, but it feels good."

I knew you'd like it. You're always content when I'm touching your cock.

"Not *just* when you're touching my cock," I huffed. "I like it when you touch me in general."

That makes me laugh considering your reaction the first time I touched you.

"Well, I was an ignorant asshole."

Was?

"Shut up," I mumbled, and for a few minutes we were quiet before I spoke again. "Cy, can I touch you?"

Please. You never have to ask.

I pulled my hands from behind my head and let them rest on either side of Cyrus's face.

"You're fucking handsome, you know that?" I rubbed my fingertips over his fins.

Cyrus laughed around my cock, almost spitting it out.

I am not.

"You are. I stare at your stripes constantly. And that body. You're fucking ripped. Even if you don't see it, you're sexy to me."

I meant every word. I could look at the patterns covering Cyrus's body for hours, and watching him jet through the water was hypnotic. He was a generous lover and a loyal friend. Him coming into my life had changed everything. Had changed *me*.

I'm glad you think so, darling.

My cheeks warmed like they did every time he called me that. I never wanted him to stop. I never wanted what this was between us to stop.

"I really care about you, Cy," I said, fighting back a yawn. My eyelids felt heavy, and my fingers started to slow down.

I care about you too, Reece. More than you could possibly fathom.

I didn't need him to tell me, though. He showed me with his actions every day.

"CYRUS, I BROUGHT BEIGNETS!"

The door to the bedroom burst open, and Cyrus and I bolted upright.

"Oh, holy gods," Fallon screeched as I scrambled to cover my naked body with a blanket.

My heart was racing. Fallon had caught us. The biggest loudmouth around knew that Cyrus and I were hooking up.

"Do you not knock anymore?" Cyrus hissed, his color shifting to a deep blue. "Get out."

Fallon opened his mouth to protest, but ultimately turned around and slammed the door shut behind him.

"Gods dammit." I ran my fingers through my hair.

"Reece, I am *so* sorry. He normally parties so hard that he's hungover the next day. I didn't think he'd make it back home, and he doesn't typically barge in like this."

Without saying a word, I got out of bed and walked into

the bathroom. Locking the door behind me, I collapsed on the cool tile floor.

This wasn't Cyrus's fault. I knew that. But I was angry and upset. I needed a few moments to process what had just happened.

"Reece," Cyrus whispered from the other side of the door. "Please talk to me. Don't shut me out."

"We should have just told everyone. Now they're going to hear it from Fallon."

"You don't know that. He would never intentionally do something to hurt me, and now that extends to you. We should go talk to him. And I know you love beignets."

I sat there for a few minutes, taking deep breaths and getting my emotions in check. The old me would have stormed off, or threatened the griffon with bodily harm if he muttered even one word of this to anyone else.

But I didn't want to be that person anymore.

And I did love beignets.

"Okay," I huffed and rose to my feet.

When I opened the door, Cyrus was standing there with my clothes in his hands.

He waited patiently while I dressed and once I was ready, we walked down the hall to the living area.

The box of beignets sat on the counter and the sliding door to the terrace was open.

"I am so so sorry," Fallon chirped the moment Cyrus and I joined him on the outdoor sofa. "I'm not used to you having anyone over, and gods, Reece was the last person I expected. I knew you guys were getting close, but I didn't know it was like this."

I worried my lip a second before reaching over and grabbing Cyrus's hand. "We, uh, we've been seeing each other for a few months now. We—I— was waiting for the right time to go public with our relationship."

Fallon fluffed his feathers and nodded his head. "I respect that, man."

"We'd appreciate it if you kept this quiet for now. Just until Reece is ready." Cyrus gripped my hand tighter and gave me a soft smile.

"Whatever the two of you need. I freaking knew something was going on with you, Cy. All the paint—"

Cyrus cleared his throat, and Fallon clamped his beak shut.

All the paintings?

"Anyway." Cyrus rose up on his tentacles. "Why don't we dig into those beignets and I'll make us some coffee, hmm?"

"Yeah, sure." Fallon stood and started to follow Cyrus inside. "But just so you know, the image of Reece's cock is like, burned into my brain. You're fucking hung, man," he quipped to me over his shoulder.

Cyrus whipped around and glared at Fallon, his thin lips pulled back and his sharp white teeth bared. "If you value your life, stop it right now," he hissed. His body was already darkening to that blackish-blue hue it took on when he was angry.

Fallon certainly knew how to push people to their limits.

"Hey, man. We're cool, we're cool. I was just trying to lighten the mood. It'll never happen again." Fallon shrank down to the floor submissively, almost like a scolded dog.

Cyrus blinked several times and took a deep breath, his color slowly fading to its familiar teal blue as he relaxed.

You would think I'd be afraid of Cyrus when he acted like that—that possessive, dominant version of himself—but it fucking turned me on. If Fallon wasn't here, I'd beg him to spread me over the island and have his way with me.

It would have to wait for another day, though.

The three of us moved inside without another word, the tension in the room heavy.

Cyrus set to work starting the coffee, and Fallon sat down on one of the barstools around the island. His feathers laid flat against his body and his tail hung limp behind him.

I patted Fallon's back, offering the griffon some comfort before sitting down next to him at the counter. "It's alright, bud. He didn't mean it."

Cyrus turned away from what he was doing and stared at Fallon. "I'm sorry I overreacted. But in the future, please don't talk about the impressive size of Reece's," he thought for a moment, "*equipment*, in front of him like that."

My cheeks burned.

The *impressive* size of my equipment.

Holy gods.

I reached across the island and pulled the box of beignets closer to Fallon and me. "Alright, then. Well. Now that we've gotten that awkward conversation out of the way, let's eat."

TWENTY-THREE

Cyrus

"Do you think Fallon's said anything?" Reece asked through the phone. "I feel like everyone has been acting pretty much the same."

"I think he's kept good on his word. He hasn't even made any jokes about it."

"That's shocking, but I mean, he probably doesn't want to piss you off. You're scary when you're angry."

I laughed. "I am not. You think it's sexy."

"I do, but if we weren't fucking I'd be terrified."

We both laughed and then went quiet.

"How are you feeling about tomorrow?" I asked.

The triathlon was the following morning, and we'd decided it was best if Reece slept in his own bed and kept to his usual routine. I had this annoying habit of distracting him with sex.

"Eh, I'm a little nervous." It was late in the evening and I could hear him rustling around on his bed, getting comfortable. "But, uh, I'm looking at the race differently now."

"Differently how?"

"I think I've been going about this the wrong way. This is my first triathlon. I'm competing against monsters and humans that have done this before. Realistically, I'm not going to be the best. But I can be *my* best. I'd like to finish in under ninety minutes. With my training times, it's definitely possible, as long as my transitions don't slow me down."

This was it.

It wasn't just the swim time Reece had been working on improving, but his mindset.

"I am so proud of you. It's nice to see you letting go of that 'if you're not first, you're last' mentality."

"I'm trying." I heard the rustling of his blankets again. "I'm feeling antsy. I wish you were here—so we could do the thing."

"The thing?" I asked, knowing full well he meant cockwarming, but wanting him to say it.

"Cockwarming," he mumbled under his breath, like he was embarrassed someone would hear him.

It was his latest obsession, and I loved the comfort I was able to provide him by doing it.

"Well, I'm not there right now, but I know something else you can do to work out that stress. You could use your tentacle friend."

I'd ordered Reece that tentacle dildo and he'd yet to keep good on his end of the bargain.

"Do you think it's a good idea the night before a race?" He sounded both intrigued and hesitant.

"It isn't any bigger than my tentacles. And I believe it was Pliny the Elder that said 'athletes when sluggish are revitalized by lovemaking.'"

I heard him moving around his room. "Well, if pine tree says it."

"Pliny, not pine tree!" I laughed. "He was a Roman

scholar. Why don't you get yourself set up and video call me back?"

"Alright. Did you, uh, have any special requests?"

My good boy was always so eager to please.

"You know what I like. Talk to you soon."

"Bye."

The moment I heard the call disconnect I grabbed my laptop, setting it up on the nightstand and tilting it toward the headboard so Reece would be able to see me. I wasn't going to have him fuck himself with his dildo without offering anything in return.

I pulled my stroker out of the nightstand and after about ten minutes, Reece initiated the video chat.

"Can you see me okay?" he asked. His face was so close to his webcam that it filled the entire screen.

"Yes, I can see you," I laughed and leaned against my headboard. "You can move back a bit now."

Reece dug his teeth into his lip before stepping away from the screen.

He was dressed in nothing but a navy blue athletic thong, the tight globes of his ass devouring the thin piece of material with each of his steps.

"Gods damn," I huffed.

My mate was breathtaking.

From what I could tell, he was in his bathroom, with the blue-green tentacle dildo suctioned to the tile floor.

"Do you like it?" He did a few poses, flexing his muscles.

"I fucking love it." My mating tentacles were already tingling, begging to play. "Get your lube and warm yourself up a bit first. Show me how you play with yourself when I'm not there."

Reece started to slip the thong down his waist.

"No, no. Leave it on. Just push it out of the way," I instructed, my eyes focused on the strain of his thick cock against the fabric.

He snatched the lube from the counter next to him and lowered down in front of the camera. With a snap, he popped open the lube and squeezed a generous amount into his hand.

His eyes were shut, his lips parted with tiny groans as he palmed his cock using his unlubed hand.

"That's right. Pull it out for me, let me see you."

Reece shifted the material to the side, letting his dick and his balls slip loose from the confines of the thong. He spread the lube up and down his shaft with rough strokes, the wide vein on the top bulging with each pass.

My mating tentacles throbbed with need as I recalled how he felt inside my mouth, how it felt being inside of him.

"Yes," I groaned.

My eyes remained glued to the screen, taking in the beauty of my mate as my tentacle circled the entrance of my stroker.

"More?" Reece asked, his voice husky.

"Yes, more."

Again, the cap of the lube snapped and Reece applied it to his fingers. He adjusted his position, pulling the thong to the side, giving me a better look at his entrance. With two fingers, he circled his hole, coating it with lube before easing his fingertips inside.

"Fuck." He threw his head back with a moan, then watched me with hooded eyes.

My mate liked watching me as much as I enjoyed watching him.

I pulsed in and out of my stroker. My tentacle writhing and twisting, wishing I was fucking Reece, wishing I was there to bring him the pleasure that only I could.

"Good boy. Fuck yourself with your fingers. Get ready for your toy," I praised.

Reece scissored his fingers, stretching and prepping before adding a third.

"Stroke your cock with your free hand," I commanded, my voice stern.

"Gods dammit, Cy," he whined. "I'm going to come before I get on the dildo."

"Shh, you'll be alright. Nice and slow. Stroke that pretty cock for me, darling."

His free hand gripped his cock, jerking it with lazy strokes while he finger fucked his ass.

"Good boy. You're so obedient. Are you ready to use your toy?"

I was getting close myself, and I knew it wouldn't take Reece long to come once he got on top of the dildo.

"Yes, gods yes." He slowly pulled out his fingers and positioned himself over the tip of the tentacle dildo.

While the color resembled mine, that's about where the similarities ended. For this, though, it would do.

"Ready?" Reece asked, those green eyes staring at me through the webcam.

"Yes, nice and easy."

Slowly, Reece began to lower himself onto the tapered tip of the tentacle, his thighs spread wide so I had a clear view as it disappeared inside of him.

"Shit," he hissed, rocking slightly and taking the dildo deeper.

"How does it feel?"

"So good," he panted.

"Do you want to come?" I already knew the answer.

"Please."

I loved it when he begged.

"Bounce for me and jerk off." My eyes were glued to the screen, watching Reece's every move while my tentacle bored into the stroker.

"Cyrus," he groaned. His strong hand stroked his cock and his body pulsed on the dildo. "Gonna come."

"Come for me, darling. Give me your cum."

Reece grunted and tightly gripped his cock, his body convulsing as thick streams of cum shot out onto his hand.

"Yes. Fuck, yes," I moaned, my tentacle flooding the silicone channel with cum.

"Gods damn." Reece grabbed a towel, using it to wipe his hands before rising off the dildo on stiff legs. "It's alright but not nearly as good as the real thing."

He tucked his cock back into the thong and stretched out on the floor in front of his laptop.

"Oh, thank gods. I was worried it was going to replace me."

"Nothing could ever replace you."

His heavy eyelids. The dreamy tone of his voice.

I hoped my mate actually felt that way and this wasn't just post-orgasm bliss talking.

As much as I was dreading it, I'd have to tell him soon. Regardless of the possibility of rejection, he deserved to know the truth.

It would have to wait, though. With the triathlon tomorrow, he didn't need any additional stress.

"Feeling better?" I asked as my tentacle slid out of the stroker and wriggled against a towel.

"Much better. I still wish you were here, though." He let out a long yawn.

"I wish I was, too. But I'll see you bright and early

tomorrow. You should take a shower and get some rest, darling; three A.M. will be here before you know it."

"Thank you for helping me relax, Cy. I'll see you tomorrow."

"Goodnight, Reece."

"Goodnight." He gave me a sleepy smile and then closed his laptop, ending the chat.

I stared at the black screen and a rush of feelings overwhelmed me.

It was a confusing mixture of giddiness, anxiety, and adoration.

Reece Rollins wasn't just my mate.

He was the love of my life.

TWENTY-FOUR

Reece

I pulled out my phone and read his text message one last time.

Cyrus: I know you're probably nervous as all get out, but you're going to do great. I'm so proud of you and how far you've come. I'll be there in a bit to cheer you on. *kiss face emoji*

I'd texted him back a kiss emoji with a stupid smile on my face. I don't think I'd ever get tired of hearing that he was proud of me.

Gods, I wished he was here.

He was right, I was nervous.

The oatmeal I'd eaten three hours earlier sat in my stomach like a lead weight, and I'd taken more trips to the bathroom than I cared to admit.

Since this was my first triathlon, I'd arrived at the lake two hours early to make sure my transition areas were properly set up. With my improved swim time, they'd be the main setback when it came to my ninety-minute goal.

The cool fall air stung my nostrils as I spread a towel over my transition area, using my bags to keep it from blowing away. Overnight, the temperature had dropped significantly. I'd be thankful for the extra layer of insulation from my wetsuit during the swim portion of the race.

The triathlon course was set up in a loop. We'd start at the beach with the swim portion, transition to our bikes and do the 20k ride back around to the beach, then run 5k circling back to the lake.

I was just about to start my warm-up when I heard "Reecie!" ring out across the beach. The other competitors turned their heads and stared in the direction of the noise.

My support crew was here.

Atlas, Tegan, my mother, Fallon, Jimenez, and Cyrus made their way down to the shore. Over their jackets, they were wearing safety orange t-shirts emblazoned with 'Team Reecie.' Fallon wore his like a bib around his neck, and in Cyrus's case, the shirt had been cut into a short crop top that just barely covered his chest.

My cheeks were hot with embarrassment, but it was endearing in a way. All of these beings, my friends and my family, had shown up to support me.

"You, uh, weren't kidding about the t-shirts," I grumbled as Atlas wrapped me in one of his rib-crushing hugs.

"I tried, bud," the wolven mumbled before pulling away.

"We wanted you to be able to see us!" Tegan smiled and held out her arms for a hug.

"I'm assuming Reecie was your contribution?" I asked, hugging my sister tightly.

"Of course it was. I came up with the idea and mom

made them. Gotta let everyone know you aren't quite the hardass you act like you are."

Things between Tegan and I had really improved over the last few months, and interacting with her like this never failed to warm my heart. It made me realize how much I'd missed being a part of her life.

"Oh, look at my babies! One is getting married and the other is about to race in his first triathlon!" Our mother shrieked and joined us in our hug.

Jeez, Ma. Way to rub that in.

Racing in a triathlon sort of paled in comparison to marrying your fated mate.

Reluctantly, she let us go and I walked over to greet Fallon, Jimenez, and Cyrus.

I'd felt slightly awkward around Fallon since he'd walked in on us and seen my cock, but as far as Cyrus and I could tell, he hadn't let a single word slip. He was probably scared of pissing Cyrus off.

"Uh, thanks for showing up to support me."

Javier shook my hand and pulled me into one of those bro hugs they all loved so much. "Wouldn't miss it, boss man."

Fallon ruffled his feathers, his tail flicking back and forth. "Gotta come out and support our friend."

Cyrus gave me a warm smile.

We stared at one another for a moment before I held my hand out, welcoming him into a hug just like Jimenez had done with me a few moments before.

To everyone else, it would seem innocent enough, but I needed the comfort his touch provided me.

"You're going to crush that ninety-minute goal. I know it," he murmured before I stepped away.

"I, uh, I gotta get warmed up. I'll see you at the finish

line." I scrubbed a hand over the back of my neck and smiled at my group of supporters.

"Good luck, Reecie!" Tegan beamed, and the group of them waved me off to start my warm-up.

I LINED up with the rest of the competitors on the beach, waiting for the race to start.

My heart was pounding.

A lifetime of physical fitness.

Three months of training.

It had all led up to this moment.

I didn't have time to dwell on my anxiety, though. The sound of the whistle rang out over the beach and a sea of bodies beelined towards the lake.

It was organized chaos as I jumped into the water. I did my best not to focus on everyone around me, setting my sights on the buoy, and starting to swim.

With steady kicks and sure strokes, I shot through the water, propelling myself forward with a speed that three months ago, I wouldn't have been capable of.

Cyrus had worked so hard for this.

I'd worked so hard for this.

Regardless of the outcome, as long as I gave it my all, that's what mattered.

That was something to be proud of.

TWENTY-FIVE

Cyrus

I stood next to Tegan in the spectator area, watching with bated breath as Reece hit the buoy line and swam back toward the shore. His form and his focus were spot on today, and even as a first-time participant, he'd broken away from the group early.

"He's doing amazing. All that training is really paying off. How's his time, Cy?" Tegan asked, her hands white-knuckling the metal partition in front of us. The anticipation and excitement on her face was endearing, and knowing it was all for her brother made my heart swell.

I grabbed my stopwatch and checked the timer I'd started the moment the whistle blew. "He's on pace to complete the swim in seventeen minutes. That's one of his better times."

My mate was doing so well.

He'd come so far over the last three months, and not just with training. His personal growth, his acceptance of monsters, our relationship—it was awe-inspiring.

"Go, Reece!" Atlas howled, his deep voice bellowing across the lake.

Reece continued to push himself, swimming hard and fast back to the shore.

He bolted out of the water on shaky legs, heading straight for his bike in the transition area. I held my breath as I watched him struggle with the leash for his wetsuit zipper.

I knew that this was the part of the race that was going to give him the most trouble. Even with as many timed drills as we ran, it was nothing compared to the adrenaline and fatigue of the actual race.

"Come on, Reece. Come on," I mumbled under my breath and checked the stopwatch. Every second he fought with the wetsuit put him farther away from his ninety-minute goal.

His fingers finally caught on the leash, and I shouted out his name.

Reece stared in our direction, spotting the bright orange T-shirts, smiling wide as he put on his bike gear.

"That damn wetsuit," his mother hissed and shook her head.

"It's alright." I watched Reece pedal off to start the 20k bike ride. "He'll make up for it with the bike and the run. They're his strongest events."

"Oh, for sure. He's got this in the bag," Fallon chirped and ruffled his feathers. "It'll be thirty minutes or so before they circle back around, right? I think I'm going to go grab a hot chocolate. It's freezing."

"I'm in. I can't handle the cold," Jimenez said.

"I'm good, thanks." I was too on edge for a hot chocolate, or to do anything other than stand and wait for my mate.

"Tegan, Mom, do you want to check out the snack stand? We have some time." Atlas looked at them expectantly.

"That sounds lovely, Atlas. I'll treat." Reece and Tegan's mother patted the wolven's arm affectionately.

Gods, she was adorable.

"I think I'll stay here and wait with Cy if that's okay." Tegan gave me a soft smile. "But you can bring me back a hot chocolate if it's not too much trouble."

Atlas leaned over and nuzzled his nose against her face. "You got it, baby."

The group walked off to the concession stand, leaving Tegan and me standing alone.

We were silent, our eyes glued to the road, waiting for any signs of the competitors.

"Thank you," she said quietly.

"It was nothing, really. Your brother is an impressive athlete."

Tegan turned to face me, her freckled cheeks and nose flushed red from the cold. "No, not just for that. I don't know what's going on between the two of you, but ever since he started training with you, he's been different. It's like—you've fixed something that was broken inside of him. This is the happiest I've seen him in a long time, and I think it has something to do with you." She threw her arms around my neck, wrapping me in a tight hug. "So, thank you."

I stood there, stiff and in shock, before belatedly hugging her back.

Obviously, I knew that Tegan's relationship with Reece had improved, but I never expected her to associate me with the changes she'd seen in him.

Atlas had sworn to Reece that he wouldn't say anything, and I trusted my friend.

But maybe Reece and I were giving away more than we thought.

She pulled away and wiped the corners of her eyes. "Sorry, I just never thought I'd see the day where my brother was comfortable around monsters."

"I'm very proud of him."

She smiled and nodded her head. "Me too."

TWENTY-SIX

Reece

"Motherfucker," I groaned through a mouthful of energy gel.

The shit was so sugary, but I needed to take it now if I wanted to have energy for the run.

I washed it down with a long drink of water, slammed my water bottle back into the holster, and pedaled like my life depended on it.

It wouldn't be long before the road curved back around to the beach and I'd do my second transition. My wetsuit was a major pain in the ass for the first one, eating up a good bit of the progress I'd made with the swim, but it was alright.

I was still on pace to make my ninety-minute goal.

The road opened up around the bend, and I could see the bike racks and the spectator area. I could just barely make out Cyrus and Tegan standing next to one another in those obnoxious shirts.

I dismounted and locked eyes with them while I jogged my bike over to the rack.

"Go, Reecie, go!" Tegan shouted.

"Yes, Reece!" Cyrus whooped, with several of his tentacles flailing around in the air.

My muscles were screaming, but seeing them standing there together, waiting for me, *supporting me*, it encouraged me to keep pushing.

There were a few other competitors in the transition area as I rushed to slip on my running shoes and snap on my number belt.

Exhaustion was setting in, but this was the last leg.

I could do it.

MY CHEST BURNED with each breath and my legs teetered beneath me.

I was twenty minutes into the run, and I was hitting a wall.

"Gods dammit," I huffed as a minotaur jogged past me.

I'd come so far, so fucking far, and I was going to shit the bed on the run, the part of the race that was arguably my strong suit.

The finish line had to be close.

The finish line where my friends and family would be waiting for me.

Where *Cyrus* would be waiting for me.

We'd spent three months preparing for this moment. He'd taken time out of his life to prepare me for this, to make me the best I could be.

Gods, I wanted to see him.

I wanted to hold him in my arms and tell him all the ways he made my life better.

All I had to do was get to the finish line, and he'd be right there.

I dug deep, focusing on my breathing and my running technique, willing myself to move, knowing that with each step I took, I was closer to Cyrus.

Eventually, the finish line came into view, and just like I thought, Cyrus was there.

I never thought I'd say it, but I was so fucking thankful for those gods awful shirts.

I started to sprint, pumping my legs and my arms, doing whatever I could to propel myself to Cyrus faster.

My toes crossed the finish line, but I didn't stop until I reached him.

"Reece! You did it!" he yelled over the commotion around us.

But my goal, the ninety minutes, it didn't matter right now.

Cyrus was all that mattered.

I stumbled forward, wrapping my arms around him and burying my face against his neck, uncaring that we were surrounded by our family and friends.

Everything in the background seemed to fade away, until it was just me and Cyrus standing there.

"Are you alright?" he whispered against my temple. "Everyone is staring at us."

I looked up at him, my chest heaving as I caught my breath. "Let them stare."

I was so fucking tired of hiding our relationship and letting my fears control me.

So, without a second thought, I kissed him.

Cyrus groaned into my mouth, his hands tangling in my hair as his lips parted for me, our tongues brushing against one another with slow strokes.

It wasn't our usual frantic kissing. It was more sensual, more romantic.

But we were brought out of the moment fairly quickly.

"Gods damn," Jimenez said with a whistle.

I pulled away from Cyrus and narrowed my eyes at Jimenez. "You got a staring problem, Jimenez?"

He smiled wide. "Nope. But I one hundred percent called this."

I grabbed Cyrus's hand and looked at everyone gathered around us. "It's about time we tell the rest of you that Cyrus and I are in a relationship. We've been seeing one another for a while now."

"Thank gods," Atlas and Fallon said in unison.

Tegan stared at Atlas, her mouth hanging open. "I thought something was going on! You knew and didn't tell me?"

"I'm so sorry, sweet thing, but I promised I wouldn't say anything until Reece was ready." That was enough to pacify my sister.

Fallon held his head high, his tail happily swaying in the air behind him. "I didn't say anything either, but damn am I glad the cat is out of the bag. I suck at secrets."

Cyrus laughed. "We know."

"Oh, this is so wonderful. Come here, honey." My mom stepped forward, pulling Cyrus and me into a tight hug.

She was almost as bad as Atlas, *almost*.

A breeze whipped past and goosebumps popped up along my bare arms, reminding me that I was still post-race and dressed in nothing but my tri-suit.

"Come on, let's get you changed before you catch a cold," Cyrus said, eyeing the goosebumps with concern.

"Yeah, you go with Cyrus and we'll get your gear packed up." Atlas was always so fucking kind. He really was the perfect mate and husband for my sister.

"Are you sure? But I need my ba—"

"I have it right here." Tegan unclipped my keys and handed them to Atlas before passing me my bag. "Now go."

Cyrus gripped my hand tight and led the way over to the changing stalls. "Well, that was certainly an impressive finish."

"I'm so sorry. I was hitting a wall and the only thing that pushed me through was thinking about you and then when I saw you..."

He looked over at me and smiled, those piranha teeth gleaming in the morning sun. "I'm really what pushed you through?"

"You were the only thing that mattered. Not the race, not the ninety minutes, just *you*."

Cyrus slipped inside the changing stall, pulling me inside with him.

"Really, Cy? I mean the crop top is absolutely doing it for me, but right after the race?" I asked with a laugh.

"Shh," he mumbled, pulling me tight to him. "I just wanted to do this."

Cyrus pressed his lips to mine, giving me another tender kiss.

He slowly pulled away. "Okay, now you can get dressed."

I shimmied out of my tri-suit and Cy whistled once I was fully undressed.

"Are you still coming over today?" he asked.

I slowly pulled up my sweats. My muscles were already feeling tense. "Yeah. I'm going to run home and drop my stuff off and then I'll be over."

"Perfect." Cyrus leaned close, his soft lips grazing my ear. "And I'll make sure I hold onto this crop top for you, darling."

TWENTY-SEVEN

Cyrus

Today was the day. After Reece kissed me and announced our relationship in front of everyone, I owed this to him.

I owed him the truth.

Today I was going to tell Reece that we were mates. Fallon was going out after work, so we'd have the apartment to ourselves.

I waited for Reece to arrive, anxiously pacing the hallway, my nerves too on edge to sit still.

How was he going to take this?

What if he pinned our entire relationship on the fact that we were fated mates?

What if he didn't want this—*want me*—forever?

I was certain I'd die.

There was a knock at the door, and I shuffled down the hall, uncaring if it seemed like I was waiting for him.

I opened the door and Reece greeted me with a smile. He was dressed in a hoodie and gray sweatpants, his hair still wet from showering. "Hey."

"H-Hi," I stammered. "Come in."

Reece walked inside the apartment and up to me, his

hand skating along my waist and over my backside as he brought me in for a kiss.

He pulled away and stared at me, a deep furrow etched between those perfect light red brows. "Everything okay, Cy?"

Shit.

"I think we should talk."

"If this is about what happened after the tri, I told you I was sorry. I know I should have checked to make sure you were okay with me—"

I cut him off before he could continue. "Gods no, darling. This is about something else. Something I've been meaning to discuss with you for a while now, but I wasn't sure how."

Reece grabbed my hand, twining our fingers together as much as my webbing would allow. "Please tell me."

My hearts raced and my tentacles clenched tight to my arms. As uncomfortable as the conversation was going to be, I had to do it.

But maybe I could show him exactly what it meant to be my mate.

Show Reece precisely what he meant to me.

"Come on, I want to show you something."

I held his hand tight as we walked down the hallway to the studio.

The rays of the fall sun seeped in through the windows, tinting the room a light orange.

It was fitting. It reminded me of Reece's hair.

We stood side by side in front of the windows, our hands still locked, quietly looking over Briar Glenn.

"Do you remember when we first met at the party?" I asked, my voice a hollow whisper.

"Of course I do. I'll never forget."

"Do you remember when my tentacle reached out and touched you?"

He huffed and shook his head. "Cy, I've told you time and time again I'm sorry for how—"

"No." I turned to face him. My tentacle coiled around his forearm, wrapping us together. "When it touched you, it activated my mate response. I—I almost came, right there on the spot. In front of you, in front of everyone. It was completely unexpected." My voice wavered. "Reece Rollins, you are my mate."

He was silent, his mouth hanging open slightly as tears formed in the corners of my eyes.

I let go of his hand and moved toward the row of canvases lined up against the opposite wall. Paint-splattered drop cloths covered the finished pieces.

"After your reaction to my touch, I felt defeated. Hopeless over the fact that my mate found me repulsive. I came home after the party, and for the first time in months, I painted."

I pulled the drop cloth off of the largest canvas, unveiling the painting of Reece and the merman. The very first painting I did of him.

Reece walked over until he stood directly in front of the painting. "That's me." He ran his fingers over the human's light red hair with gentle strokes.

"It's you. They're all you." Tears streamed down my face and my voice was a strained whisper as I shuffled along the row of canvases, uncovering all of them for Reece to see.

He stared at the paintings, obviously shocked.

They were a tribute to him. A series of paintings of Reece wet after the pool, Reece petting a dog, the coffee shop we frequented, Reece emerging from the lake after a swim. In one way or another, they all focused on my mate.

My everything.

"Cyrus, they're beautiful." He was crying too, his lips crinkled into a smile.

"You like them?" I asked, wiping my eyes.

"I *love* them. Come here."

I scuttled over as fast as I could and Reece wrapped me in a tight hug, his muscular arms pulling me as close to him as he could.

"And I'm in love with *you*, Cy," he said softly against my skin.

"Really?" I sniffed, glancing up at his handsome face. "You aren't freaked out about the mate bond?"

He shook his head. "Not one bit. What Atlas and Tegan have, what *we* have, I'd be crazy not to want this. It just means you won't be able to get rid of me."

I laughed and pressed my lips to his. "I love you too. Very much." I gestured toward the paintings with a tentacle. "If you couldn't already tell."

Reece's hand darted out, his fingertips tracing over the merman in the painting. "Is—is this how you wish you looked?"

He knew me too well.

"Yes. I—I thought that if I was a handsome merman, I'd have a better chance with you. That it would be less of a shock you were mated to a monster."

He took my face in his hands, sliding them just underneath my fins, and pressed his nose to the flat plane of mine. "I happen to think you're handsome just how you are. I'm lucky to have a mate with a toe-curling British accent, who's a talented painter, a bossy swim coach, and is kind to everyone he meets." He lowered his voice. "Not to mention the tentacles."

It felt like an eternity had passed since I'd met Reece

and done that first painting. Hearing how he felt about me and the way I looked through his eyes, *it made me feel confident*.

Reece rubbed his nose against mine. "Was that all you wanted to tell me?"

I nodded, then tilted my head to claim his mouth with a kiss.

After making out for a few moments, Reece pulled away with a chuckle. "As turned on as you make me, can we maybe just relax in bed today? I did race in a triathlon this morning."

"Yes, yes. Sorry. Where are my manners? Come on."

I grabbed his hand and pulled him across the hall to my bedroom.

Reece peeled back the covers before slipping into bed with a yawn.

"Do you want me to do the thing?" I asked as I climbed into bed next to him, tucking my tentacles beside me on the mattress.

"Not right now, but um, could you hold me for a bit? Just until I fall asleep?"

I loved this shy, sensitive side of him that he reserved just for me.

"Come on then."

Reece shimmied closer and I wrapped my arm around him as he snuggled against my chest. My webbed fingers settled over his hip, rubbing soothing circles until his breathing began to slow.

This was everything I'd wanted.

Everything I'd spent the entirety of my long life hoping for.

"Cy," Reece mumbled.

"Yes, darling?"

"Are you going to have to bite me, like Atlas did with Tegan? Because with your teeth I don't think that's a very good—"

Laughter rumbled out of me. I was glad that out of everything I'd just told him, *that* was his main concern. "No, kraken mate bonds are different. It's more of a mental thing."

"Huh, that would explain all the dreams I've had about you then."

I'd never really thought about it until that moment, about how the mate bond between a kraken and a human would manifest itself, but it made sense.

"It very well could be. I wish I had more answers for you."

"S'okay. But, um, Cy, are you putting those paintings in a show?" he asked.

Shit.

With everything that happened today, that little detail had slipped my mind.

"Well, I had planned on it, but I completely understand if you don't want me to."

My hand stilled, awaiting his response.

"No, I want you to. I want everyone to know. I'm proud of them. I'm proud to be your mate."

I leaned over and kissed the top of his head.

"I'm proud to be your mate too."

WHEN LIGHT SNORES slipped out of Reece, I carefully got out of bed, doing my best not to wake him, and shuffled over to the studio.

He'd caught on to the painting of the merman and the

human so easily, knowing how I felt about myself without me even saying a single word.

In truth though, I didn't see myself that way anymore.

I mixed a palette, gazing at my stripes and patterns as I blended the perfect combination of colors.

There was no way that painting was going on exhibit looking like that.

For hours, while Reece slept, I painted.

I'd glance at myself in the mirror then use my paintbrush to recreate my image on canvas.

When I was finished, I stepped back to take in the final piece.

While I'd left Reece unchanged, the merman had been replaced with a perfect rendition of myself. A beautiful blue-green kraken with a billowing parachute of tentacles below his waist embraced his human mate underwater. They stared at one another lovingly, knowing that they'd make the journey back to the surface—together.

It was perfect.

I knew my mate would think so too.

Reece

EPILOGUE

One Month Later

"I look like a fucking college professor," I huffed, checking my outfit in the mirror.

Tonight was Cyrus's art show, and I'd made the mistake of letting him dress me for the event.

He'd chosen a burnt orange sweater layered over a gingham button-down, dark wash jeans, and some sort of blazer-jacket hybrid.

It was out of my comfort zone, that was for sure.

Cyrus came up behind me in the mirror, resting his head on my shoulder and wrapping his arms around my waist. "I think you look quite handsome. You can't wear gray sweatpants everywhere." He turned his head, his soft lips grazing the shell of my ear as he whispered, "Even if your cock looks fab in them."

I curved my arm upward, rubbing my fingertips over the delicate fins along Cyrus's neck as I stared at the two of us in the mirror. "I love you so much, you know that?"

A wide smile spread over his face. "I love you, darling.

But we'll see if you still feel that way when we're in a room full of people eyeballing a painting of your ass."

I let out a deep sigh as he pulled away, knowing exactly which painting he meant. The one he'd painted the day we met, the one of me and the merman.

I wasn't sighing because of my ass being on display, though, I was sighing because it killed me that Cy didn't see his beauty the way I did.

"Did you confirm your therapy appointment," he called out from his bedroom.

"Yes," I yelled back as I straightened a few out-of-place hairs. "Confirmed for Thursday at five."

It was a long time coming, but I was finally committed to resolving the issues from my childhood with the help of a trained professional.

"Reece, we're going to be late."

"Are we still staying at my place tonight?" I asked as I followed Cyrus out into the hall.

Over the past month, we'd been spending most of our free time together, alternating between Cyrus's place and mine. I was hoping to change that soon.

"Yes, yes. Why do you keep asking that?" He tilted his head, raising the bumpy protrusions above his eye that served as eyebrows. "Are you up to something?"

Motherfucker.

I was gods awful when it came to surprises.

"You're just gonna have to wait and see." I turned away from Cyrus to hide my smile and grabbed my keys from the console table. "Let's roll."

We held hands as we walked across the parking lot to my car. It was one of the perks of being open about our relationship. I could touch Cyrus anytime I wanted.

I slid into the driver's seat with Cyrus sitting beside me

in the passenger seat. "You're going to have to navigate because I have no idea how to get to Rock Harbor from here."

Cyrus snorted. "Reece, you just helped me take paintings to the gallery the other day. You really don't remember how to get there?"

"Nope. You know I space out when I'm in the car."

"That's comforting, considering you drive around Briar Glenn for work. I'll navigate, but can you put some music on?" Cy asked, one of his tentacles tapping impatiently.

I connected my phone to Bluetooth and started the music. The sound of Robert Smith's voice filtered out of the speakers and filled the car.

"What's this?" Cyrus asked. He reached over the center console and grabbed my hand. "I thought you didn't like my sad boy shit."

I shrugged and pulled out of the parking lot. "Guess your taste in music is rubbing off on me."

The forty-five-minute drive to Rock Harbor passed quickly, with Cyrus telling me stories about his time in England and what it was like when he met Atlas and Fallon for the first time.

Compared to humans, he'd lived so many lifetimes. I tried not to think about what that meant for us in the grand scheme of things, but I needed to know what to expect.

"Cy," I said, pulling the car into a parking spot and shutting off the engine.

"Yes, darling?"

"I, uh, I wanted to ask you. Now that we're mated, what happens to you when I die? You know, because your lifespan is so long."

His grip on my hand tightened. "Well, I don't have a lot of information to go on, but I'd assume our life forces are tied together in some way. You'll live slightly longer, and I'll live a much shorter lifespan as your mate. But I don't think we'll ever have to experience life without one another. When you go, I go."

As sad as it was that Cyrus's lifespan would be drastically shorter because I was his mate, it also brought me comfort in a way. I'd never have to worry about how he'd cope without me.

I leaned over the center console and ran my hand along his jaw, pulling him in for a kiss.

"I love you," I whispered against his lips.

"I love you too. Now, let's hurry inside before Eduardo loses his shit."

"ABOUT TIME," Eduardo huffed the moment we walked through the gallery doors.

The bright white space was filled to the brim with humans and monsters, all admiring Cyrus's artwork.

"Sorry we're late. There was traffic." Cyrus hugged Eduardo, then kissed both of his cheeks.

"Mhm, I'm sure there was." Eduardo looked me up and down. "Well, don't you look handsome? He cleans up nicely, Cyrus."

I tugged at my collar awkwardly and Cyrus grabbed my arm, easing some of my discomfort. "He certainly does. Now if you'll excuse us, I'd like to show Reece around. We'll catch up with you later."

With that, Cyrus put his hand on the small of my back and led me away from Eduardo.

"What is it with that guy?" I mumbled when we were far enough away.

"He's jealous of you. He tried to pursue me in the past, but I shot him down. It probably kills him that you're my mate."

"You never told me Eduardo was into you."

"I thought it was obvious, and you're my mate. It isn't like it matters. Come here, I want to show you something."

Cyrus led me through a sea of people, occasionally stopping to introduce me or chit-chat, until we arrived at an alcove in the back of the gallery.

"Come on." Cyrus unclipped the velvet rope partition securing the area and ushered me inside.

"What is this?" I asked as we walked down a bright hallway.

"Close your eyes," he whispered and grabbed my hand.

I followed his instructions, walking blindly alongside him until he pulled me to a stop.

"I wanted you to be the first one to see this piece, so I had Eduardo set it up back here. Open your eyes."

My eyes fluttered open, taking in the painting in front of me.

It was the one Cyrus had painted the first time we'd met. The one of me underwater, my bare ass on full display, but this time it was different.

Instead of a merman embracing me, it was Cyrus.

"It's you," I said quietly, my fingers tracing over his blue-green stripes and delicate fins.

"It is. I painted over it the night of the triathlon. Am I handsome enough for you?"

I turned to face him, wrapping my hands around his waist and holding him tight. "You'll always be handsome enough for me."

Cyrus

EPILOGUE CONT.

"Gods, I can't wait to get out of these clothes," Reece said the moment we walked through the front door of his house.

We'd put a lot of finishing touches into his place over the last month, and it was quickly becoming my favorite space to spend time with him. Sure, I loved the apartment with its view and the terrace, but I loved the privacy of Reece's house more.

"Mmm." I wrapped my arms around him, my mating tentacle uncoiling from my arm to lightly caress his throat. "I can't wait to get you out of those clothes either."

"Always so horny." He snorted. "You're gonna have to wait though. I want to show you something first."

"Well, this is just a night full of surprises. We are truly one of those sickeningly cute couples."

He rolled his bright green eyes and grabbed my hand. "Shut up. Come on."

Reece led me through the kitchen and over to the side door that led to the garage.

"If you got me one of those wagons you attach to the

back of a bike, I'm going to throw a fit. I already told you I'm not riding—"

"Cyrus! Stop! Close your eyes."

I shut my eyes and Reece led me down the steps into the garage.

"Open," he instructed.

The whole garage had been emptied and covered with a fresh coat of white paint. Windows were installed along the exterior wall, allowing sunlight to filter into the space during the day. Canvases lined the opposite wall, and there was a utility cart fully stocked with painting supplies.

"Do you like it?" He pulled me into the center of the room.

"You did this for me?"

He pursed his mustache down over his lip and nodded. *My handsome grumpy walrus—who was much less grumpy these days.*

"I love it, Reece."

It was true. It was the most thoughtful thing anyone had ever done for me.

"Atlas helped me with the windows, but I did all the rest. I, uh, I was wondering if you wanted to move in with me." He gave me a hopeful look, his cheeks blushing bright red.

Gods, he was everything.

I lunged at him, wrapping my arms and my tentacles, whatever I could, around him and hugged him tightly. "I would love to move in with you."

We'd discussed getting married at some point, but we wanted to let Atlas and Tegan have their moment first. Moving in together was the next logical step, and I was thrilled that Reece had taken matters into his own hands.

"I love you, Cyrus," he whispered, his hands traveling down my back to where my tentacles began.

"I love you too. Now, why don't we get you undressed so I can fuck you in *our* house for the first time?"

We'd be happy here.

Together.

Me and my mate.

ACKNOWLEDGMENTS

Conky- Thank you for making another beautiful cover, chapter headers, and everything else you do for me. You're a phenomenal artist and a fantastic friend. I'm so glad you're a part of my life. I love you!!

Kristen- I don't think I would have completed this book without your help. Thank you for always being there for me and assisting me with anything I need. You are one of my best friends and you have the best GIFs. I'm so lucky to know you.

Lindsay- You keep my life organized and I'm infinitely grateful. Thank you for putting up with my scatterbrained, overwhelmed self. You da best, bb.

Meg- I <3 Meg! All of your work on the Discord server is so appreciated. Thank you for featuring all of us indie monster romance authors in your calendar! You can check it out here.

TORRI, Wendy, Sierra, Sarah, Stephanie, Mimi, Kenzie, Kassie, and Kendra- Thank you for being a bomb alpha/beta reading squad! You helped make this book amazing and gave me the confidence I needed to finish it up. I love you all!!

To the Cryptid Canva Cunts, you drug me over the finish line with this one. Thank you for being the best friends and the most encouraging beings I've ever met. My days are a lot less lonely (and more productive) with the three of you in my life.

The Beignets- You are the most uplifting and supportive individuals I know. Thank you for believing in me and my writing. I love all of you so much, and I'm lucky to have you in my life!

ABOUT THE AUTHOR

Ashley is an avid reader and during the Covid-19 pandemic, she decided to dip her toes into writing and hasn't looked back. She loves coffee, candles, fall weather, mid-century modern furniture, and a good alien romance (complete with fancy peens).

Connect with Ashley <u>here.</u>

<u>Purchase signed copies here!</u>

For access to exclusive content and merchandise, <u>join me on Patreon.</u>

MANTRAS & MINOTAURS

LEVIATHAN FITNESS #3

Click here to preorder book #3 in the Leviathan Fitness series!

Made in United States
Troutdale, OR
03/02/2024

18147916R00126